DOCTOR WHO AND THE
BRAIN OF MORBIUS

Also available in the Target series:

DOCTOR WHO
AND THE
BRAIN OF MORBIUS

Based on the BBC television serial *The Brain of Morbius* by Robin Bland by arrangement with the British Broadcasting Corporation

TERRANCE DICKS

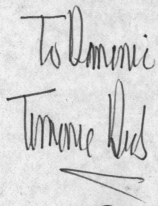

A TARGET BOOK
published by
the Paperback Division of
W. H. ALLEN & Co. Ltd

A Target Book
Published in 1977
by the Paperback Division of W. H. Allen & Co. Ltd
A Howard & Wyndham Company
44 Hill Street, London W1X 8LB

Reprinted 1978, 1979, 1981

Printed in Great Britain by
Hunt Barnard Printing Ltd, Aylesbury, Bucks.

ISBN 0 426 11674 7

Contents

1

A Graveyard of Spaceships

Kriz was dying.

Painfully he dragged his insect-like body away from the blazing ruins of the shattered spaceship. Only a powerful survival instinct kept him alive and moving. Two of his legs were broken, and he scrabbled painfully across the razor-sharp rocks with the remaining four. The tough, chitinous carapace that covered his body was cracked clear across, and thick purplish blood welled sluggishly from the wound, leaving a glistening trail across the rocks behind him.

Kriz paused, swinging his huge head with its shining, many-faceted eyes. Behind him he could see the ship, its body as buckled and shattered as his own by the savage impact of the crash. Black smoke was pouring from the wreckage. Even as he watched there was a sudden red glow, and a shattering explosion as the fuel-chamber of the Zison-drive blew up. The rilium plates twisted and buckled in the fierce blaze, molten metal running over the rocks. Dimly Kriz felt that the life-blood of the ship, like his own, was pouring away onto the rocks of this bleak alien planet.

Painfully Kriz crawled on. His dying mind was still full of the moments before the crash. It had been a routine exploratory flight. Kriz came from a world where his insect-like species had evolved into the dominant race. Their deep-seated instincts for order, co-operation and selfless hard work had built a great civilisation. Kriz, like all his people, existed only to serve the Race, which in turn was symbolised by the Nest, and by the Great Mother, Goddess and Queen in one. The Race had only one problem—lack of living space. As Nest after Nest was established, the home planet became impossibly crowded, and they sought always for new worlds to colonise. Not to conquer, for Kriz's people were a moral race. Planets too harsh to sustain other species, worlds devastated by the wars in which other life-forms so often destroyed themselves, were taken over and made habitable by the technology of the Race.

This had seemed just such a world. Orbiting the planet on his preliminary survey, Kriz had seen nothing but ruin and desolation on his scanners. A world of mountains and rocky deserts, barely able to sustain life. A few ruined buildings suggested a civilisation once powerful but now vanished. Kriz remembered his growing feelings of exaltation. Surely this was another home for the Race ... Then *something*, some incredible *force* had seized his little scouter and smashed it down at the foot of this mountain range.

Kriz struggled on. He had no very clear idea where he was going and he sensed that even if he found help, he was too badly hurt to survive. But while he lived, he would struggle. It was not in the nature of the Race to surrender.

On the mountain slope just above him, a massive

figure leaped ape-like from rock to rock, moving ever closer. Condo, attracted by the smoke as a vulture is drawn by blood, was stalking his prey. Satisfied there was no danger, he rose to his full height, a massive figure in rough leather garments. He steadied himself against the rocks with the steel hook that took the place of his left hand.

Should he wait till the creature was dead? Even though wounded it could still be dangerous. Sometimes those who survived the crashes carried weapons ... Condo rubbed a scar on his massive forearm. He growled impatiently, deep in his throat ... It might take the creature many hours to die. If Condo moved quickly enough ... He drew the heavy, short-bladed sword from his belt, running a grimy thumb along the razor-sharp edge. Suddenly he bounded forwards, following the blood-trail across the rocks.

Kriz's failing senses gave him no warning of the hunter's approach. Suddenly the massive figure was *there*, looming above him. Feebly Kriz moved two of his fore-limbs in the Intergalactic signals that offered peace, and begged for help. He saw the shining blade in the newcomer's hand, and realised that here was no help—only death. Kriz gave a high-pitched whistling scream of distress. The blade flashed down, and his pain was over.

Condo bent over the body, dragging a grimy sack from inside his jerkin. Minutes later he straightened up, thrust the sword back in his belt and bounded away across the rocks. He carried a round, sacking-wrapped bundle beneath one arm.

Darkness was falling as he made his way across the

barren, rocky landscape. There was a distant rumble of thunder, an occasional lightning-flash. Condo shivered with superstitious fear. Solon, his master, had told him time and time again that the frequent sudden storms were a purely natural phenomenon. But to Condo they were the work of the black-robed Sisterhood, weaving their evil spells in a temple deep in the mountain caves. Apart from Solon himself, the Sisters were the one thing on Karn that Condo feared. Perhaps it was because he sensed that, in spite of all his denials, Solon feared them too.

There was another lightning flash, a louder crash of thunder. Great spattering drops of rain began to fall. Condo increased his already headlong pace, hoping to reach the shelter of the building he called the castle before he was hit by the full fury of the storm. Deep in his savage heart he believed that the Sisters summoned up the storm, riding on the night-winds like great bats in their long black robes.

He came to the castle at last, an immense towering structure that dominated the end of a narrow valley. So huge was the edifice that it seemed to merge with the towering mountain range behind it. The ramparts and terraces, the broken towers and shattered turrets, stretched up and up against the lightning-streaked blackness of the sky. The place would have given most people the screaming horrors, but to Condo it was home.

He padded lightly across the broken drawbridge. It was never raised now, nor could it be, since the complex electronic machinery that controlled it was long since rusted and useless. Condo set his shoulder to the great main door. Slowly it creaked open, revealing the shadowy depth of the great hall. Solon was working in the little pool of light cast by one of the fossil-fuel lamps. On the stone table before him was the head-and-shoulders clay bust of a humanoid, with high, domed forehead, arrogantly jutting nose and a great square jaw. It was a face for a king and emperor. Condo watched silently as Solon's long slim hands caressed the still-wet clay. Solon had made and re-made the bust a hundred times, always creating the same face. Always he destroyed his efforts and began again, muttering that it was 'Not right, not right ...' Condo stood waiting, not daring to speak.

Solon hated interruptions when he was engaged on this seemingly endless task, and Condo feared to provoke one of his sudden, terrible rages.

Solon stepped back, frowning with dissatisfaction. Still gazing at the bust, he said suddenly, 'You were quick, Condo. Did you find survivors?'

Condo jumped. 'One—oxygen-breather.'

'Excellent. Quick, quick, let me see.'

Fumbling in terror, Condo passed over the sack. Solon groped inside and pulled out the head of Kriz, severed cleanly at the neck. He held it up. Kriz's sightless, many-faceted eyes seemed to glow in the light of the lamp. Solon examined the head, moving it closer to the lamp. 'Oh, no, no, no. That won't do. No, even if the ganglia could be re-connected ... the cranium is too narrow, the development of the cerebrum totally different.' He held the severed head up against the clay bust. 'Look—it's an *insect*! Even a half-witted cannibal like you can see it won't do.'

He flung the head down in disgust. It rolled across the table and thudded to the floor. Condo cringed away. 'But the big-heads not come, master. Not come to Karn.'

Solon's eyes gleamed. 'They will, Condo. One day ... One day a true humanoid will come, warm-blooded with a compatible nervous system. *One* such specimen, just *one*, and I can complete my work.'

Condo touched the head with a booted foot. It rolled a little further. 'Not want?'

Solon sighed. 'Oh, take it to the laboratory. I can always use it for experiment.' As Condo gathered up the head and crept from the hall, Solon returned to the bust. His voice was low and yearning. 'One day, Morbius, I promise. One day ...'

A wheezing, groaning sound filled the night air of Karn, merging with the occasional rumblings of thunder. A square blue shape materialised out of the air. In outward form it was a police box, of the kind once used in a country named England, on a distant planet called Earth. Inwardly it was something very different—a Space/Time craft called the TARDIS.

The door opened and a very tall, very angry man sprang out. He was casually dressed in a loose comfortable jacket and trousers, with a battered, broad-rimmed hat jammed on to a tangle of curly hair. An extraordinarily long scarf was wound round his neck. He shook his fist at the lowering night sky and shouted, 'All right! Come on out! Just show yourselves, I dare you!'

A slender, dark-haired girl followed him out of the TARDIS. She was carrying a big torch which she shone round the unfriendly-looking landscape. She shuddered, not very favourably impressed by what she saw.

The Doctor ignored her, still addressing his unseen adversaries. 'Meddlesome interfering idiots,' he bellowed. 'I know you're there somewhere. Come out, I say!'

There was no reply. Just the constant rumble of thunder, the howling of the night wind. 'Messing about with my TARDIS, dragging us a thousand parsecs off course ...'

The girl tapped him on the shoulder. 'Have you gone potty, Doctor? Who are you shouting at?'

The Doctor looked round impatiently. 'My dear Sarah, the Time Lords, who else?' He glared round indignantly. 'And now, you see? You see? They're out there listening and they haven't even the courtesy to show their noses!'

Sarah sniffed. 'I don't wonder. Probably afraid of getting them punched, the way you're carrying on.'

The Doctor stamped up and down, muttering, 'Intolerable! Well, I won't stand any more of it!'

Sarah looked thoughtfully at him. At times like this, she realised she knew very little about the Doctor, and even less about his mysterious superiors, the Time Lords. She'd first encountered the Doctor when he was working as scientific adviser to an organisation known as UNIT—the United Nations Intelligence Taskforce. Sceptical at first, she had finally come to accept that the Doctor was a being from some other

13

planet, with the ability to travel in Space and Time. She had even seen him change his physical form, becoming literally a new man, in order to overcome the effects of a near-fatal dose of radiation.

As for the Time Lords, Sarah knew only that they were the rulers of the Doctor's own mysterious race. Long, long ago the Doctor had apparently quarrelled with them, fleeing his home planet to roam the Universe in his TARDIS. The Time Lords had hunted him as a fugitive, captured him and sentenced him to exile on Earth. Eventually there had been a kind of uneasy truce. The Time Lords had restored the Doctor's freedom to travel in Space and Time. In return they expected him to carry out occasional missions for them, invariably of a hideously dangerous kind. Limited as it was, the Doctor still resented this interference with his freedom, and never accepted a mission without furious protests. To counter this, the Time Lords sometimes dropped the Doctor right into the middle of a perilous situation, confident that his curiosity, and sense of justice, would force him to discover what was going on, and so do their work for them.

Another possibility occurred to Sarah. Nodding towards the TARDIS, she interrupted the Doctor's tirade. 'Why can't it just have gone wrong again?'

The Doctor whirled round indignantly. 'What?'

'The TARDIS. After all,' added Sarah unkindly, 'it wouldn't exactly be the first time, would it?' Miracle of technology though it was, the TARDIS did have an undeniable tendency to be erratic. Take its present shape, for example. The TARDIS was *supposed* to change its appearance to blend in with the surroundings. In a forest it should look like a tree. Here, it should have taken on the appearance of one of the surrounding rocks. Unfortunately this Chameleon mechanism' had long ago jammed, and the TARDIS now arrived on alien worlds in the constant guise of a London police box.

This was only a minor inconvenience. More serious were the undoubted faults in the TARDIS's guidance circuitry. Although it could travel in Space and Time, the TARDIS had an awkward habit of delivering its passengers to the wrong planet or the wrong century. Was this what had happened now? Clearly the Doctor didn't think so. 'Don't you think I know the difference between a simple error and outside interference? Oh no, there's something going on here, some bit of dirty work they won't touch with their lily-white Time Lord hands.' Again the Doctor raised his voice. 'Well, I won't do it, do you hear?' He raised his face to the sky, and shook a defiant fist. A very large raindrop came down and hit him in the eye. There was another rumble of thunder, louder and nearer this time.

Sarah looked up at the night sky. 'That sounds ominous. Where do you think we are?'

The Doctor sat down on a rock. 'Don't know. Don't really care.'

'Oh, come on, Doctor, stop being childish.'

'I am not going to move, Sarah. I'm just going to sit here and do *nothing* ...'

'... so there!' completed Sarah. And indeed, the Doctor sounded exactly like a sulky child.

The Doctor refused to be laughed out of his bad temper. He hunched his shoulders and pulled his hat down over his eyes. More scattered raindrops fell, huge splashy ones that seemed to hold a good cupful of water each. One landed on Sarah's nose, and she wiped it away with the back of her hand. 'We're going to get awfully wet soon.'

Loudly the Doctor said, 'Bah!' and relapsed into silence.

Sarah swung round the torch. As far as she could make out they were in some kind of hollow in the rocks. If she climbed to the rim, she could get a better look around them. Suddenly a gleam of white caught Sarah's eye and she scrambled across to it. Lying at the foot of one of the rocks was a white plastic globe about a metre in diameter. It had been partially smashed open, and resembled, thought Sarah, a giant table-tennis ball that had been stepped on by a giant foot. Despite its size the thing was incredibly light. She picked it up and carried it across to the Doctor.

'Hey, look what I've found! What is it?'

The Doctor peered from beneath the brim of his hat. 'Ejection bubble,' he said dismissively.

'It's a what?'

'Space parachute.'

Sarah studied the plastic sphere, trying to work out how it was used. Presumably you shut yourself inside it, and got shot out through some kind of automatic ejection chute. 'So someone's had a crash?'

'Apparently.' The Doctor was still refusing to get involved.

Sarah dropped the ejection bubble, made her way

across the little hollow, and climbed the low rim at its edge. A sudden lightning flash lit up the area before her and she gasped in astonishment.

The plain was littered with wrecked spaceships. Sarah guessed there were at least a dozen of them, in all shapes and sizes, all stages of decay. She jumped down and ran back to the Doctor.

'There must be a dozen wrecks out there, Doctor, It's like a graveyard of spaceships.'

So determined was the Doctor to go on sulking that even this extraordinary news aroused only a flicker of interest. 'Fancy that.'

'It's incredible. Why should they all have crashed here?'

'No idea.'

'Well, I think we ought to take a look, Doctor. It might have something to do with the reason *we* crashed.'

The Doctor fished something from his capacious pockets. To her astonishment Sarah saw it was a Yo-Yo. Impatiently she said, 'Well, are you coming?'

The Yo-Yo flashed up and down in the Doctor's hand. 'No, I'll just sit here and practise my backward double loops.'

'Please yourself. I'm going anyway.' Sarah began moving off. She stopped, hesitated. Despite her torch, the night seemed very dark. 'You're *sure* you're not coming?'

Intent upon the acrobatics of his Yo-Yo, the Doctor made no reply. Sarah shrugged, and set off into the darkness.

Left alone, the Doctor went on practising for a few

2

minutes. But his heart wasn't in it. He was already beginning to feel rather ashamed of his childish behaviour, and even the achievement of a particularly fine backward double loop didn't make him feel any better. He put away his Yo-Yo and stood up, intending to stroll casually after Sarah. Suddenly a piercing scream split the darkness, and the distant gleam of Sarah's torch went abruptly out. The Doctor sprinted towards her.

He found Sarah crouched at the foot of a jagged pinnacle of rock, her face in her hands, the smashed torch at her feet. Nearby lay a huddled shape. The Doctor knelt to examine it. Without looking round, Sarah said, 'I suppose ... it was the crash?'

The Doctor examined the headless body, noting the cracked carapace, the way in which the neck had been severed in one clean stroke. 'No. Not. in the crash. This happened afterwards.'

Sarah shuddered. 'You mean someone deliberately cut off ...'

The Doctor was trying to reconstruct the sequence of events. 'It looks as if he had tried to escape in the ejection bubble, and was badly hurt in the landing. Then somebody, or something, attacked him.'

Sarah risked a quick glance at the insect-like body. 'What was it?'

'One of a mutant insect species,' said the Doctor abstractedly. 'Widely established in the Nebulae of Cyclops.' He was gazing skywards. 'I thought those stars looked familiar.'

'You've been here before?'

'I was born somewhere in these parts.'

'Near here?'

'Well, within a few billion miles or so.'

Sarah stood up. As much to get away from the headless body as anything else, she climbed a little higher in the rocks. Her back to the spaceships' graveyard, she was gazing in the other direction when another lightning flash lit up the landscape. In the distance it revealed a long narrow valley, with an enormous building dominating the far end. 'Doctor, look,' she called.

The Doctor climbed up beside her. They waited for a further lightning flash, and she pointed out the towering building.

The Doctor nodded thoughtfully. 'I think we'd better take a look at it, Sarah.' He glanced down at the headless corpse. 'There's something very nasty going on here.'

Quite oblivious to the fact that the machinations of the Time Lords had ensnared him once more, the Doctor set off towards the castle. Sarah followed him. 'Well, at least there's some kind of civilisation.'

The Doctor looked down at her. 'There was a civilisation,' he said ominously.

A sudden rainstorm began lashing down. The Doctor felt in his pockets. 'You're not going to start playing with that silly Yo-Yo again?' demanded Sarah.

The Doctor gave her a reproachful look and produced a stubby cylinder. With amazing speed it expanded into a sizeable umbrella. Holding it over them both, he led the way towards the castle.

Neither the Doctor nor Sarah saw the black-cowled figure, watching their departure from the shadow of a nearby rock. As they moved away, it hesitated for a moment then scurried off in the other direction.

Their arrival had been observed by the Sisterhood of the Flame.

The Keepers of the Flame

The storm was at its height now. The night winds howled about the castle, sheets of rain lashed against its crumbling towers. In one of them a light glowed from a window. Solon was at work in his laboratory.

Inside the room the noise of the storm was fainter, muffled by the thick stone walls. The laboratory was in semi-darkness, illuminated only by an electric globe that cast a fierce beam of light onto the bench. There, neatly wired into a complex metal grid, was the severed head of Kriz. Using a long metal stylus, Solon was delicately touching controls in the base of the grid, sending minute electrical impulses into the dead brain. With each touch the head twitched into a ghastly pseudo-life. The eyes rolled, seeming to glare wildly round the room. The mouth opened in a horrible parody of a smile.

To anyone else the sight would have been one of sheer horror, but to Solon it was utterly absorbing. Intent upon his work, he scarcely noticed the raging of the storm.

He turned from the grid to record the results of his experiment in the huge leather-bound ledger that lay on the bench. Just as he began to write, the electric globe flared brighter for a second, then went out. Solon cursed fluently, but the emergency was a routine one, and he was well prepared. The rusty generators in the basement seldom worked for long at a time, needing constant patching up to keep them going. Solon reserved the erratic power supply for his scientific work, making do with more primitive lighting for everyday needs.

Fishing in the pocket of his robes, he produced a stub of candle and a match, which he scraped against the nearest wall. There was a flare of yellow light, and Solon lit the candle, holding it high above his head.

The flickering yellow glow illuminated the rest of the room, playing across dusty benches stacked high with tottering piles of electronic equipment, most of it half-dismantled. As Solon made his way across the room, the candlelight fell briefly on a huge, old-fashioned four-poster bed that occupied one corner. Scarlet drapes on all four sides turned it into a kind of tent. Solon paused for a moment, and gazed yearningly at the four-poster. Then he made his way to the door. 'Condo, bring lamps at once! Condo, where are you?'

As if in response to Solon's voice, the scarlet drapes around the bed suddenly billowed outwards, as though disturbed by a wildly-flailing limb. Solon called again. 'Condo, you fool, where have you got to? Lamps, I say!'

Muttering angrily, Solon left the laboratory and began heading towards the stairs. The drapes became still again, and the laboratory subsided into darkness. Beneath the noise of the storm, another sound could be heard. On the shrouded four-poster bed, *something* was breathing hoarsely.

The black-robed figure glided silently across the rocky face of Karn, seemingly immune to the howling winds and lashing torrential rain. It came at last to a dark cave mouth in the mountainside, and passed silently inside. The cave led to a tunnel, and the tunnel wound down and down, deep into the heart of the mountain. Every now and then torches flamed and smoked in holders set into the rocky walls. The torches seemed to flare brighter as the black-robed figure passed by.

In a kind of ante-chamber, the figure paused and removed its outer robes. It was revealed as a woman, with a smooth beautiful face that had an ageless quality. The woman who stepped forward to take the cloak, younger still in appearance, had exactly the same quality in her face. So indeed did all the Sisterhood. From the moment of Initiation, time was suspended for them. They aged no further, living forever as servants and keepers of the Flame—so long as they continued to consume the Elixir of Life.

Dismissing the junior Sister with a gesture, the woman passed through the antechamber and into the Temple beyond. Her name was Ohica, and she was a Priestess of the Flame. The Temple was a small circular chamber, a kind of amphitheatre. Its focal point was the pair of ornately decorated bronze gates set into the far wall. Behind them burned the sacred Flame of Life, so holy that it could be revealed only during the secret ceremonies of the Sisterhood. All around, black-robed figures kept a silent vigil.

Before the gates, on a rocky protuberance that formed a natural throne, sat a small wizened figure. This was Maren, High Priestess of the Sisterhood. Her face was seamed and wrinkled with an incredible weight of years. Ironically, Maren had already been old when the Secret of the Elixir was first discovered. Time was suspended for her, as for the other Sisters, but for Maren eternal life meant eternal old age.

She listened silently as Ohica described the square, blue object that had materialised, the two strangely dressed people who had left it and headed for Solon's castle.

When Ohica had finished, Maren nodded slowly. Her voice was little more than a whisper. 'Two of them, you say?'

'A male and a female, Maren.'

Maren shook her head in disbelief. 'Our senses reach beyond the five planets. And they were not seen.'

Ohica's voice was firm. 'Yet they are here.'

Perhaps because of her great age, Maren was always reluctant to accept anything new. 'No ship can approach this planet without detection,' she croaked proudly. 'Even the silent gas dirigibles of the Moothi I *felt* in my bones, while they were still a million miles distant.'

'There *was* no ship, Maren,' said Ohica patiently. 'The last was the scout-ship of the insect race.'

'Then how, Ohica? *How* did they come?'

'I do not know, Maren. I say only what my eyes have seen.'

Maren gazed into space, her bright eyes fiercely alive in the incredibly old face. 'Can it be as I have feared? For months I have been haunted by a premonition, that *they* would send someone to take the Elixir from us.'

Slowly Maren rose to her feet. With an imperious hand she waved the other Sisters out of the Temple. Once they were gone, she turned back to Ohica. 'Next to myself, you are the senior of our Sisterhood. Come, let me show you what the others must never know.' She hobbled across to the bronze gates, unlocked them with an enormous key produced from beneath her robes, and flung them back.

Behind the gates was an alcove in the wall, in which was set a shallow basin carved from the solid rock. It resembled an old-fashioned drinking fountain. But from the vent in the centre of the basin flowed not water but fire. A small flame no more than six inches high flickered in the still air. Below the flame, a silver chalice rested in a stone holder cut into the rock.

Instinctively Ohica bowed her head in reverence. 'The Flame of Life!' Then she gasped, 'Maren, what is wrong? Why is the Flame so low?'

There was infinite sadness in the old voice. 'The Flame dies, Ohica. Every day it sinks a fraction lower.'

Ohica's mind was reeling under the shock. 'How can this be? At our ceremonies the Flame has burned brightly, higher than our heads.'

'Deception, my child. For many months I have secretly fed the Flame with powdered rineweed.'

'Then we are doomed? Our Sisterhood will perish?'

'We are but the Servants of the Flame, my child. If the Flame dies, so must we.'

The two women looked silently at each other, both sharing the same terrible thought. To lose life is bad enough—but to lose *eternal* life ...

Hesitantly Ohica said, 'Should not the others be told?'

Maren shook her head. 'No! Not until our end is certain. I have thought long upon this ...'

Closing the copper gates that shielded the Flame, she hobbled painfully back to her seat. After a long brooding silence she began to speak. 'As you know, the secret of the Elixir of Life that we draw from the Flame is known only to our Sisterhood, and the High Council of the Time Lords. Since the time of the great destruction, when first they aided us, we have shared the Elixir with the Time Lords.'

'And now there is none to share?'

'The few phials that are left I have kept for ourselves. One fear now fills my mind—that the Time Lords will rob us of these last few precious drops.'

'You think the two I saw have been sent to steal the Elixir?'

Maren rose to her feet. 'If they have, then we shall destroy them. Summon our Sisters, Ohica. We shall form the Circle.'

Ohica struck a gong that hung beside the throne. Silently, the black-robed Sisters began filing into the Temple.

Since Condo failed to respond to his yells and threats,

Solon was forced to go and find his own lamps. Naturally enough, the ones he found were empty, and he had to make the long trip down to the cellars where the fuel-oil was kept. He was in a savage mood by the time he returned to the great hall—to find Condo rummaging in a vast iron chest that stood by the wall.

The huge barbarian jumped back guiltily as Solon stormed into the hall, an oil-lamp in each hand. The lid of the chest fell with an echoing clang. Solon set down his lamps and advanced menacingly on his giant servant. 'Well, and where have you been?'

Condo hung his head, rather like a small child being told off, but made no reply.

'Answer me, you stupid ox,' snapped Solon. 'Where have you been?'

Condo scratched his chin with his hook, trying to think up an acceptable excuse. Finally he grunted, 'Me look for food, Master.'

'A lie! You can't deceive me, Condo. You were looking for that arm, weren't you?'

Condo nodded guiltily.

'I've told you before, Condo, you'll get your arm back when our task here is finished, and not before.'

Condo bowed his head. 'Yes, Master.'

Solon looked at him with a self-satisfied smile. This was only the latest of many such conversations. When the slave ship carrying Condo had crash-landed on the planet, the huge barbarian had been the only survivor. However, his left arm had been almost severed in the crash. While Condo was still un-

27

conscious, Solon, for purposes of his own, had removed the limb completely, replacing it with a crude bionic arm ending in a metal hook. As soon as he became aware of this, Condo began pestering Solon to give him his own arm back. Solon soon realised that the missing arm gave him a tremendous hold over Condo. The promise that one day the arm would be restored kept the big barbarian humble and obedient.

Even Condo realised that in escaping from the crash to become Solon's servant he had simply exchanged one form of slavery for another. In his savage heart he hated Solon, and often planned to kill him. But while there was a chance the missing arm would be restored to him, Condo was powerless to rebel.

Solon was well aware of his servant's feelings, and took a sadistic delight in his power over Condo. 'Serve me well and I'll put it back, as good as new, but if you fail me ...' He grabbed Condo's hook and held it high in the air. 'Fail me and you'll keep this hook for the rest of your life. Understand?'

Condo nodded meekly—and there came a sudden jangle from the rusty bell that hung outside the main door. Solon swung round in alarm.

'The door—someone ring,' growled Condo, never one to avoid the obvious.

Solon glared at him. 'I'm aware of that. Answer it, fool.'

Condo lumbered across to the main door and heaved it open. Immediately the oil lamps flared as wind mixed with rain swept through the hall. In the doorway stood two extraordinary figures, a tall man in a floppy hat and long scarf, and a slender girl. Despite the umbrella the tall man held over them, both were soaking wet. Outside, lightning flashed, thunder rumbled, and lashing rain poured down.

Condo stared at them in puzzlement. 'What you want?'

The Doctor smiled. 'May I have a glass of water?' Realising that his little joke was lost on the slow-thinking Condo, he slipped nimbly past him and into the hall. Sarah followed.

They found themselves confronting a medium-sized man in flowing robes that somehow suggested the academic. His smooth face was not unhandsome—but Sarah immediately felt there was something un-trustworthy about it—a suggestion of slyness, cunning, treachery. The man was staring at them. 'Humans,' he breathed. 'Humans, at last.' Suddenly he seemed to collect himself. 'Condo, what are you thinking of? Let them in, close the door.'

Condo slammed the door, and the noise of the storm died down. Solon bustled forward, an ingratiating smile on his face. 'My dear sir, my dear young lady! You've no idea what a pleasure this is. It's been so long since we had visitors. Condo, take their things! You must eat, drink, rest ...'

Sarah broke into this flood of hospitable chatter. 'If we could shelter here for a while—then we'll be off. My name is Sarah Jane Smith, by the way. And this is the Doctor.'

Solon wouldn't hear of their leaving. 'Great heavens, this is no night to be travelling. I wouldn't dream of letting you proceed another step. Stir yourself, Condo, our guests are cold and tired. Let me take your hat, sir.'

The Doctor removed his hat, which by now was little more than a lump of sopping wet felt, and handed it to Solon. Solon took it and stepped back, gazing up at the Doctor in admiration. 'Your head,' he whispered. 'Oh, what a *magnificent* head!'

The Doctor was a little taken aback by this rather fulsome compliment. 'I'm sorry?'

Solon was still staring up at him. 'Quite, *quite* superb!'

The Doctor smiled modestly. 'I'm glad you like it. I've had several,' he said chattily. 'I used to have an old grey model before this one. Some people liked it.'

Sarah grinned, wondering what their host would make of all this nonsense. 'Well, I was very fond of it,' she whispered.

The Doctor smiled down at her. 'So were a lot of people,' he conceded. 'But I think I prefer this one!'

Once again, Solon seemed to come to. 'I *beg* your pardon. What a surly host you must think me. *Do* please come and sit down and get warm. Condo, see to the fire. Bring food and wine!'

Condo raked the smouldering logs with a massive poker and a sulky flame appeared. Solon waved him away, and ushered the Doctor and Sarah to a table near the fire, dragging forward heavily carved chairs. Sarah stretched her hand out to the flame. 'You're very kind,' she said, feeling a little overpowered by Solon's effusive hospitality.

'Not at all, not at all. I am *honoured* to offer such comfort as my humble abode can provide. Though as you can see, the amenities here are somewhat primitive.'

As Sarah looked round the huge draughty hall, she was inclined to agree with him, though she was too polite to say so. 'Oh no,' she protested, 'I think it's all very nice.'

Solon beamed at her. 'Now, I want to hear *all* about your adventures. I have so few visitors here on Karn.'

The Doctor nodded. 'We're on Karn, are we? I should have known.'

Solon looked puzzled. 'You mean you arrived here *without* knowing?'

The Doctor frowned, reminded of the Time Lords' intervention. Hurriedly Sarah said, 'Sometimes we go on a sort of mystery tour, don't we, Doctor?'

The Doctor was looking at the clay bust that stood on a nearby side-table. 'You seem very interested in heads, Mr ... ?'

'*Doctor*, actually. Doctor Mehendri Solon.' Solon spoke quickly, and Sarah felt the title was very important to him. He hurried forward and flung a cloth over the bust. 'I dabble in modelling a little—this one's not very good, though.'

'You're too modest, Doctor Solon. The strange thing is, I seem to recognise that head.'

The Doctor made as if to remove the cloth, but Solon stepped hurriedly in front of him. 'Oh, no, I'm sure you're mistaken.'

The Doctor gazed thoughtfully at Solon. Like Sarah, he felt there was something very odd about their host, something that made him uneasy. He

31

decided to probe a little further. 'Speaking of heads, or rather their absence, we found a headless body lower down the mountain.'

Solon shuddered. 'How very distressing. From one of the crashed spacecraft, no doubt?'

'Perhaps. And there's another thing. How many wrecks did we count, Sarah?'

'About fifteen, I think.'

The Doctor looked sternly at Solon. 'The wreckage of *fifteen* spaceships, all in this one area.'

Solon shrugged. 'I understand there's a localised belt of magnetic radiation.'

'Magnetic radiation?' The Doctor frowned. The term was so vague as to be scientifically meaningless.

Solon gave an apologetic shrug. 'I know little of these matters, Doctor, but I believe that *is* the theory.' With evident relief he turned to Condo, who had just re-entered the hall bearing a loaded tray. 'Over here, Condo.'

As Condo set the tray on the table, balancing it deftly between his good hand and his hook, Sarah thought him quite the fiercest looking butler she'd ever seen.

Solon was looking over the contents of the tray 'Now then, what have we here? I hope Condo's managed to find something special for us.' Sarah saw that the tray held an old and dusty wine bottle, and goblets in a metal that looked like pewter. A number of plates and dishes in the same material held a variety of rather odd-looking cold foods.

Solon picked up the wine bottle and examined it. 'Condo, you fool, how many times must I tell you?

This wine should be opened and decanted, to allow it to breathe.'

'Yes, Master.' Obediently, Condo picked up the bottle.

Solon looked meaningfully at him. *'Then do as you've been instructed. Hurry.'* As Condo disappeared with the bottle, Solon said apologetically. 'An excellent fellow, utterly devoted to me. But I fear his intelligence is not of the highest.'

Sarah couldn't help feeling sorry for Solon's strange servant. 'How did he lose his arm?'

'Many years ago I was able to save him from the wreckage of a crashed Dravidian spaceship. I do whatever I can, whenever there's a crash.' Solon sighed. 'I had to remove the arm to save his life.'

The Doctor looked up. 'I see. He's not a Dravidian himself though, is he?'

'No indeed. The ship was taking prisoners to one of their colonies.' Waving away the subject of Condo, Solon selected a dish from the tray. 'Now these blue lobsters are considered a delicacy here on Karn ...'

In the kitchen just behind the great hall, Condo pried the cork from the bottle with his hook, and poured the wine into a jug. From beneath his jerkin he produced a tiny bottle, and poured a coloured liquid into the wine. Picking up the jug, he set off for the hall.

This was not the first time unexpected visitors had arrived at Solon's castle—and disappeared, never to be seen or heard of again. Solon could always use fresh subjects for his strange experiments.

The Horror Behind the Curtain

Within their Temple, the Sisters of the Flame had formed a Circle of Power. They swayed gently to and fro to the wailing notes of some kind of flute. A low, rhythmic chanting filled the air. In the centre of the circle sat Maren, hunched over a crystal sphere gazing intently into its depths.

The ceremony was simply a device, a way of concentrating the Elixir-stimulated, extra-sensory powers of the Sisters into one combined effort. As she gazed into the crystal, old Maren could *feel* the currents of mental force swirling around her. She concentrated them, focussed them on the sphere of crystal, and a swirling mist appeared inside its depths. The mist cleared to reveal a square blue shape. Maren hissed exultantly, 'I see it. I see the machine of our enemy.' She gazed fiercely round the circle. 'Concentrate, Sisters. More power. *More power!*'

The concentration of psychic energy in the Sanctum rose to a point where it could be physically felt in the air. A whirling spot of light appeared on one rocky wall. Its glow expanded into a whirlpool, a swirling cone of brightness. A square blue shape materialised silently in at its core. Maren gasped, 'Enough, Sisters, enough. It is done!'

The chanting died down, the eerie music stopped,

the light faded—and the TARDIS stood by the wall of the sanctum. Maren rose stiffly and hobbled across to it. 'I was right, Sisters. It *is* a Space/Time machine.' Her mind groped for an almost forgotten word. 'It is a—TARDIS! Only the Time Lords have such machines as this.'

Ohica said slowly, 'Then the one I saw—*he* was a Time Lord?'

Maren nodded fiercely. 'Sent here to steal the Elixir.'

Ohica moved closer, speaking softly so that the others would not hear. 'Then what can we do, Maren? Among all the races of the galaxy, only the Time Lords are our equals in mental power.'

'That is true, Ohica. Other races we can destroy from within, we can place death in the secret centres of their being, destroy them with false visions. But against this Time Lord, such powers can have no effect. He will simply close his mind to us.'

'Then all is lost?'

Maren smiled coldly. 'No. There are other ways.' She raised her voice. 'Form the circle once more, Sisters. We have work to do.'

The robed figures returned to their places, the flute took up its wailing tune, and once again a low chanting filled the air. In the centre of the Circle, Maren focussed the build-up of psychic power within her, preparing to hurl it against the Time Lord who was their enemy.

Slowly a face began to appear in the depths of the crystal ball ...

*

Sarah waved away another plate of odd-looking delicacies. 'No thank you, I really couldn't.'

Solon returned the dish to the tray, and went on talking. He really was being the perfect host, thought Sarah. What was it that was making her feel so uneasy ... Perhaps it was Condo, looming menacingly in the background. He had stationed himself behind the Doctor's chair, and for some strange reason his eyes seemed fixed unwinkingly on the back of the Doctor's neck, while he fingered the hilt of the sword in his belt.

She became aware that Solon was still chatting on, and wrenched her wandering attention back to his words. 'Yes, one never really overcomes the nostalgia for the planet of one's birth,' Solon was saying. 'Sometimes at night I look up at the night sky and wonder ... shall I ever see Earth again.'

Sarah looked meaningfully at the Doctor. 'Believe me, I know *exactly* how you feel!'

Leaning back in his chair, apparently quite relaxed, the Doctor chose to ignore Sarah's little dig. 'Tell me, Doctor Solon, what made you decide to settle here on Karn?'

'As I'm sure you know, Doctor, Karn is a ruined planet. After the years of destruction, when the war finally ended, almost everyone moved away. Nobody lives here now, nobody bothers me. I can get on with my work in peace. Take this building—once it housed a hydrogen reactor—totally abandoned and derelict. Now I've converted it into my own private castle!'

Sarah looked round the gloomy hall. So that was it! Solon didn't really own this place. He'd simply moved in here, living like a rat in the ruins. And there was something curiously rat-like about him, come to think of it. A plump, well-fed rat, sleek and bright-eyed. Feeling rather guilty at having such unkind thoughts about her host, Sarah thought she'd better join in the conversation. 'What kind of work do you do?'

Solon seemed to hesitate, and surprisingly it was the Doctor who answered her question. 'Micro-surgical Techniques in Tissue Transplants. Wasn't that your most famous paper, Doctor Solon?'

Solon paused, looking keenly at the Doctor. 'So you know something of my history?'

The Doctor smiled. 'But of course. After all, you were one of the most gifted surgeons of your time.' He turned to Sarah. 'Which was considerably after *your* time, incidentally.'

Solon still didn't speak. He seemed taken aback by the Doctor's knowledge of his past. Cheerfully, the Doctor continued, 'You know, your sudden disappearance caused quite a stir. It was said you'd become a follower of the Cult of Morbius.'

Sarah sensed that the Doctor was testing Solon in some way—this last shot quite definitely went home. She saw Solon stiffen, and he seemed about to make some angry retort. Then he controlled himself, produced another of his rather sinister smiles and said, 'Malicious rumours, Doctor. Academic jealousy, you know. It was all very distressing. That's why I had to get away ...' (Condo sensed the change in his master's mood, sensed the anger beneath the smooth words. He edged closer to the Doctor's chair, his hand going

37

to the sword in his belt. Solon caught the movement, gave a slight warning shake of his head, and Condo backed away.)

Solon lifted the wine jug from the tray. 'Enough of this. Let's turn to more pleasant things. You haven't yet tried my wine, Doctor. I think you'll enjoy it— an excellent vintage.'

The Doctor sipped the wine appreciatively. 'From Dexos, isn't it?'

'Precisely, Doctor, the greatest wine-planet in our galaxy. Of course, the vintners have a natural advantage in treading the grapes. After all, they've each got six legs!'

Solon chuckled delightedly at his own little joke. But his eyes were cold as he watched the Doctor take another sip of wine.

(Maren glared malevolently at the face in the crystal ball. The Time Lord was leaning back, relaxed and smiling. 'So,' she hissed. 'Our enemy thinks himself safe in Solon's castle!' The chanting of the Sisters rose to a higher pitch.)

Despite Solon's recommendations, Sarah didn't really care for the wine. It was heady, and tasted highly spiced. But the Doctor seemed to like it well enough. He drained his glass, and made no objection when Solon hastened to refill it for him. Seeing that she was unobserved, Sarah discreetly tipped the rest of her wine into the debris of the lobster bowl.

Solon made no attempt to offer *her* any more wine. He seemed interested only in the Doctor. 'Drink up, Doctor. I always knew that someday I'd have a guest with a *head* for such a fine vintage.' Solon smiled again.

Suddenly the main doors crashed open, and a cold wind swirled through the room. Lamps flickered, the fire belched smoke, some of the heavy metal dishes were swept to the floor, and various small loose objects whirled through the air. Wind howled round the hall for a moment longer, then suddenly departed, slamming the door closed again as it shrieked away.

Sarah sat bolt upright, clutching the arms of her chair. 'What *was* that?'

She could see that Solon was as terrified as herself. Nevertheless, he managed a rather sickly smile. 'Oh, just a kind of freak squall. The abnormal weather conditions here on Karn, you know.'

Only the Doctor seemed undisturbed by what had happened. He was still leaning back in his chair. In fact he was positively slumped, thought Sarah. He stared a little glassily at Solon. 'A telekinetic visit, perhaps? From the Sisterhood of the Flame?'

Once again, Solon was clearly shaken by the Doctor's knowledge. 'You know of the Sisterhood?'

The Doctor nodded, tapping the side of his nose with his finger with a gesture of rather woozy cunning. He took the finger from his nose and used it to point at the little side table where the clay bust was visible once more. The sudden wind had whipped away the concealing cloth. Solemnly the Doctor said, 'I know

who that reminds me of now. Renegade Time Lord—
Morbius!'

Sarah was staring at the Doctor in alarm. 'Doctor,
are you all right?' He was acting as if he was drunk—
or drugged.

'Coursh, I'm all right,' replied the Doctor indignantly. He struggled to sit up straighter, but
couldn't seem to manage it. 'Thatsh Morbiush all
right ... One of the mosht deshpicable, criminally
minded wretchesh ...' The Doctor slumped forwards,
collapsing face-down across the table.

Sarah's mind was racing. The Doctor couldn't
really be drunk, not on two goblets of wine. Which
meant that the wine *must* have been drugged. Her
best chance of safety lay in pretending that she too
had succumbed. She let herself slump forwards,
burying her face in her arms. She heard Solon's ex-
ultant voice. 'There are some of us who hold very
different opinions about Morbius, Doctor.' Peeping
sideways, Sarah saw Solon lift the Doctor's head by
the hair, then lower it carefully to the table again.
'It worked, Condo. He is ours!'

She saw Condo step forward, a gleaming blade in
his hand. 'I take head now?'

Solon thrust him to one side. 'Clown! Put that
thing away! This will be no crude butchery. A
head such as this ... a head that will one day command
the universe ... must be removed with care and skill.
Every step will be planned, every suture, every in-
cision must be perfect. This will be my triumph,
Condo. A thousand years from now, people will remember Solon's last and greatest feat of surgery.'

'Not last, Master. Me last! You put back arm. You promise.'

Solon brushed him aside. 'Bah! Your arm is nothing. Any third-rate hack can replace an arm. But a head, the centre of the entire nervous system, a million tiny fibres ... a head demands more than mere skill, Condo. It demands genius!'

Sarah had been listening to this gruesome conversation with steadily increasing horror. Suddenly Condo grunted, 'What about girl?'

'Girl? What girl?' Sarah realised that Solon was so absorbed with the Doctor that he'd forgotten her existence.

Condo pointed. Solon said impatiently, 'Oh, her. Kill her, of course.'

Sarah saw Condo draw his sword and start moving towards her. She was tensing herself to leap up and run when Solon said, 'Not now, you fool, later. I am impatient to begin. Now, Condo, carry the Doctor to the laboratory.'

Sarah remained quite still as Condo lifted the Doctor from his chair and carried him out of the room. She heard Solon shriek, 'Mind his head, you oaf. It mustn't be damaged. Carry him *carefully* ...'

Voices and footsteps died away. Sarah waited a moment longer, then got up and slipped out of the hall after them.

Under a constant barrage of threats and exhortations to be more careful, Condo carried the Doctor along the corridor, up the stairs, along the upper gallery and into Solon's laboratory. While Solon rushed about lighting candles, Condo laid the Doctor on a bench. Solon bustled forwards, stethoscope in hand, and began examining the Doctor. 'Yes ... just as I thought. There's a secondary cardio-vascular system. He's a Time Lord right enough. This is excellent, Condo, more than I ever dared hope for. Now we can be sure there will be no problems with tissue rejection.' He rubbed his hands together exultantly, flexing the long fingers in anticipation.

Condo backed away from the Doctor in awe. 'Time Lords dangerous, Master. Much power.'

'Rubbish. The Time Lords are spineless parasites. Morbius offered them greatness and they rejected and betrayed him!' Solon's voice rose to a shriek. 'They'll pay for that mistake, Condo. Pacifist degenerates that they are, they'll be the first to suffer the revenge of Morbius!'

(Maren leaned forward and gazed into the crystal. 'Now is the moment, Sister. The Time Lord sleeps, he cannot protect himself against us. Concentrate, sisters. *Concentrate!* The chanting rose even higher, and the surge of power began to build ...)

As Solon concluded his examination, Condo wheeled forward a tray of gleaming surgical instruments. Although far from the ideal operating theatre assistant, he had attended at enough of Solon's strange experiments to give a certain amout of basic help. '*Now* we take head, Master?'

Solon waved him away. 'Do you think I'm going to

work by candlelight? I need proper lighting, power for my laser-scalpels. Come—we must repair the generator.'

As Solon and Condo made for the door, Sarah slipped back along the corridor into the concealing darkness. She'd trailed Solon and Condo to the laboratory, and watched Solon's examination. She'd formed a vague plan of distracting them into chasing her, giving the Doctor time to recover. Now she watched the two figures disappear down the corridor. They'd actually left the Doctor alone and unguarded. If only she could revive him and get him away ...

(While the Doctor lay unconscious on the bench, and Sarah was looking the other way, something very strange happened. A sudden glow of light bathed his body, and he simply disappeared.)

Sarah ran into the laboratory, stopping in utter astonishment at the sight of the empty bench. The Doctor had been *there* a minute ago, she'd seen him. And there simply hadn't been time for them to move him far ...

Sarah looked round the gloomy laboratory, illuminated only by the few flickering candles Solon had left behind. A dark shape in the corner caught her eye, and picking up a candle she moved towards it.

The shape resolved itself into a four-poster bed, with curtains all round. Sarah sighed with relief. Obviously they'd dumped the Doctor on this bed until they were ready to begin their ghastly operation. There was a flutter of movement behind the curtains. Clearly the Doctor was starting to come to. Sarah pulled back the curtain. In the gloom she could dimly see a body. 'Doctor, is that you?' she called. The figure stirred but made no reply. 'Come on, Doctor,' Sarah whispered. 'Wake up, we've got to get out of here!'

She was about to give the figure a shake when the electricity came on. The laboratory was flooded with glaring light, and Sarah found herself leaning over not the Doctor, but a monstrosity so horrible that she clapped her hand over her mouth to stifle a scream.

On the bed lay a hideous hybrid of alien life forms, a monster that was somehow made up of bits of other creatures. Fur, scales and even feathers were jumbled together in a ghastly parody of life. The left arm, for instance, was human, but on the right was an enormous claw. Worst of all the thing was clearly alive—but *it had no head!*

In unbelieving horror, Sarah saw that the Monster was trying to sit up. It flexed an arm, and the giant claw stretched out towards her ...

4

Captive of the Flame

Sarah backed slowly away from the headless Monster, fighting an instinct to scream and run in blind panic. To her enormous relief the creature slumped back on the bed, the giant claw waving blindly as if by some kind of reflex. Hastily Sarah closed the curtains around the bed.

For the first time she became fully aware of her surroundings, the laboratory now fully revealed in the bright light of the electric globes. She saw equipment-piled benches, racks and trays of brightly gleaming surgical instruments—and the head of Kriz still fastened to the metal grid. Sarah shook her own head in wondering horror. 'Solon's mad,' she thought, 'he's just got to be mad.' She glanced again at the curtain-shrouded bed. Was Solon really planning to remove the Doctor's head and somehow attach it to *that*? It was too horrible even to think about. And where *was* the Doctor? Realising that the shock of seeing the Monster had distracted her from her search, Sarah started moving around the laboratory. Perhaps there was some kind of annexe leading off, a concealed door even ... She hadn't got far with her search when she heard voices and footsteps. Solon and Condo were coming back. Hastily Sarah ducked down behind the bed, and peeped cautiously out.

Solon came into the laboratory, pausing impatiently in the doorway as Condo's clumsy fingers helped him into a surgical gown. 'Hurry, man. I must sterilise all the implements before we begin. You understand, Condo?'

'Yes, Master.'

Solon knew full well that Condo didn't understand at all, but he was so full of enthusiasm over the coming operation that he simply *had* to go on talking about it. 'You see, in this type of operation the risk of infection is very high. The slightest inflammation could totally ruin——'

The flow of words cut off as Solon caught sight of the bench where he'd left the Doctor. A guttural choking came from his throat, as sheer astonishment deprived him of the power of speech. Condo looked down in puzzlement at his master, and Solon gesticulated wildly towards the bench.

Condo looked across at the empty bench and frowned. He turned back to Solon, and once more demonstrated his mastery of the obvious. 'Doctor gone,' he said simply.

Solon was almost beserk with rage. 'Imbecile! Imbecile!' He reached up and cuffed Condo savagely across the face. 'I can *see* he's gone, you chicken-brained biological disaster! But *how? Where?*' He grabbed Condo and shook him. 'The drug—did you put *all* of it in?'

'Yes, Master. All of little bottle in big one.'

'Then he can't have gone far. Not even a Time Lord could shake *that* dose off so soon.' Solon began pacing up and down the laboratory. Suddenly he stopped, and hammered a fist down on the bench: 'The Sisterhood! That squalid brood of harpies. They've rescued him with one of their wretched telekinetic tricks! That accursed hag Maren found I was holding a Time Lord and *rescued* him.' By now Solon was almost foaming at the mouth with rage. 'May her stinking bones rot. I'll see her die yet, Condo. I'll see that palsied harridan screaming for death before Morbius and I are finished with her!'

Condo listened unimpressed to this flood of threats. He was a practical man in his simple way, and clearly shouting wouldn't help them. 'What *do*, Master?' he asked.

Solon glared at him. '*Do?* We must get the Doctor back of course. I could wait a lifetime and not find another head as suitable. Whatever the risk I *must* get him back. Come, Condo!' He bustled the big man out of the room. Sarah waited a moment, crept from her hiding place and followed them. Despite the mystery of the Doctor's disappearance, she was feeling a little more cheerful. Solon had spoken of the Doctor being 'rescued'. Surely that meant he must now be in friendly hands? Anything was better than being the captive of this mad head-chopper.

Sarah crept cautiously down the corridor. Whatever happened, Solon mustn't be allowed to get the Doctor back in his power.

The Doctor awoke to see a wrinkled old face hovering above him in misty darkness. Mind still wandering a little he asked vaguely, 'How long have I been ill, nurse?'

He saw by the frown on the old face that he'd made a wrong guess.

'I am Maren, leader of the Sisters,' she croaked angrily.

'Sorry, Matron,' said the Doctor placatingly. He must have got the old soul's rank wrong.

'My name is *Maren*. I lead the Sisterhood of the Flame—as you well know.'

The Doctor shook his head to clear it and looked around him. He was in a rock-walled chamber lit by flaring torches. Their light revealed a set of bronze gates—and the familiar shape of the TARDIS on the other side of the room. The Doctor tried to get up, and realised that he was bound hand and foot, propped up like a Guy Fawkes dummy against the foot of Maren's throne. The wizened, robed face of Maren regarded him malevolently from her throne. Other black-robed figures hovered nearby. The Doctor sighed. 'Things seem to have been happening while I was having my little nap.'

Impatiently Maren snapped, 'You feign ignorance, Time Lord?'

The Doctor smiled. 'Just call me Doctor,' he said modestly. 'I hate all this bowing and scraping.'

'You wish to confess?'

'Confess? To what?'

'That you were sent here by the High Council of the Time Lords.'

The Doctor smiled. 'Ah! Well, I must confess ...'

'Good!' Maren nodded in satisfaction.

'... that I don't really know,' concluded the Doctor. 'The calibrators *have* been on the blink—but on the other hand, the High Council are perfectly capable of interfering with the TARDIS when it suits them.' He nodded towards the TARDIS. 'How did you get the old girl here?'

Maren smiled triumphantly. 'By the Power of the Flame.'

'Teleportation? Isn't that rather a waste of psychic energy? Now if you'd get yourself a good fork-lift truck ...'

As usual in a tricky situation, the Doctor was talking nonsense to give himself time to think. But Maren was in no mood for jokes.

'Doctor, you have but a little time left. Will you waste it in babbling nonsense, or confess your guilt?'

The Doctor found there was something decidedly sinister in this last remark. 'What do you mean I have "but a little time left"?'

'*Before you die, Doctor.*'

Indignantly the Doctor straightened up. 'Nonsense! I'm only seven hundred and forty-nine. We Time Lords have a saying, life begins at seven hundred and fifty.'

'You die at sunrise. That is agreed.'

'Not by me, it isn't. I haven't even been asked.'

Maren hissed in irritation. Was there no way to make this Time Lord accept the gravity of his situation. To jest in the face of death was an offence against the dignity of the Sisterhood. She leaned forward angrily. 'Confess that you were sent here to steal the

4

Elixir of Life and your death will be mercifully swift. Otherwise it will be slow ... very slow.'

'Look,' said the Doctor patiently. 'I really haven't the slightest notion what this is all about. The last thing I remember was ...' He paused, what *was* the last thing he remembered? 'I was taking a glass of wine with Solon ... Then Morbius ...'

'Morbius is dead!' Maren was sitting bolt-upright, her eyes gleaming with anger.

The Doctor nodded thoughtfully. 'Yes, of course he is. Now, how did I get the impression ...'

'The Time Lords themselves executed Morbius for his crimes—here, on Karn.' Maren spoke vehemently, almost as if trying to convince herself.

The Doctor remembered something else. 'Solon had a clay model of Morbius's head ...' he paused thoughtfully. 'But it was more than that ... Solon drugged my wine ... Now why, I wonder ...' His voice hardened. 'Just for a second, before I passed out, there was a living mental contact. *I felt the mind of Morbius!*'

'You lie, Doctor. Morbius is dead!'

'Yet, on many planets there persists a rumour that Morbius somehow cheated death. His followers still hold secret meetings, convinced that someday Morbius will return to lead them!'

'He is *dead*, I tell you.' Maren waved a claw-like hand. 'Tell him, Ohica.'

Another of the Sisterhood stepped forward. 'Morbius was executed, for leading the rebellion, and for many of his other crimes. His body was placed in a disposal chamber and scattered to the four winds of the universe.' She spoke in a kind of ritual chant, as if repeating words that had been used so often they must be true. Obstinately the Doctor shook his head. 'I know all that. But I tell you, Maren ... Just for a second, as consciousness slipped away, the mind of Morbius touched mine. I felt his blazing hatred and anguish, the burning passion for revenge. *Morbius is alive.*'

The Doctor's words seemed to cast a chill of fear over the Inner Sanctum. Then Maren rallied. 'No doubt you think that raising these old fears will somehow aid you. But I was present at his execution. I saw him perish. Morbius is dead, Doctor ... and soon you too will die!'

On a mountain path, high outside the entrance to the caves, Solon and Condo crouched behind a massive boulder. They were watching one of the Sisters carry a huge bundle of faggots into the cave. Condo reached for his scimitar. 'Condo go down, kill?'

Solon struck his hand aside. 'Oaf! The last thing I want now is trouble with the Sisters.'

'Not kill Sisters, Master? Then how we get Doctor?'

'We wait. He's bound to come out sometime. We wait, we follow, and then when he's alone ...' Solon tapped Condo's arm. 'But not until then, you understand? And I need him alive, so I can remove his head under proper conditions.'

'Yes, Master ...' Condo tensed, looking round keenly.

'What is it? What do you hear?'

'Condo hear someone move!'

In the rocks above them, Sarah crouched motionless, hardly daring to breathe. Under cover of the darkness, she'd successfully trailed Solon and his servant without being spotted. Then, just at this last moment, she'd dislodged a tiny piece of rock with her foot, and it had rattled down the slope. The keen senses of the barbarian had picked up the tiny sound.

Solon listened a moment longer, then shrugged impatiently. 'I hear nothing—look, Condo!' He pointed to the path below. Two more Sisters were struggling along it, each carrying a heavy bundle of faggots.

Condo frowned in puzzlement. 'Why Sisters take so much wood into Temple?'

'I was wondering the same thing ...' Solon stared thoughtfully at the entrance to the cave.

Inside the Temple, the preparations were now complete. Ohica moved across to Maren, and bowed before her. 'All is ready, High One.'

Maren looked upwards. A tiny chink of light had appeared in the cavern roof high above them. 'The sun appears, Doctor. I offer you this one last chance to confess your guilt.' She produced a tiny phial from beneath her robes. 'This powder could spare you from the anger of the flame. Without it, you will die in torment. Confess!'

The Doctor sighed wearily. 'You're convinced of my guilt whatever I say. Why do you need a confession?'

'So that the Time Lords cannot deny that they have plotted against the Sisterhood.'

'Plotted against you? You've got it all wrong, Maren. The Time Lords have extended their protection to your Sisterhood for years. When Morbius attacked this planet, who was it who saved you?'

For a moment Maren was silent. Then with bitter obstinacy she said, 'They acted from self-interest—as you do now.'

The Doctor shook his head pityingly. 'I'm afraid you're confused. Still, I suppose at your age ...'

Ohica came to the defence of her High Priestess. 'The Time Lords feared Morbius, just as we did. And they depended on the Elixir of Life for their survival. Now the Elixir no longer forms, you and your fellow Time Lords want to steal the little that remains.'

'What do you mean—the Elixir no longer forms?' snapped the Doctor.

'The Sacred Flame dies—as well you know.'

'Rubbish,' said the Doctor vigorously. 'How can it die? That flame is a product of gases forcing their way up along a geological fault, right from the heart of the planet. It will burn for millions of years.'

Maren interrupted him. 'I tell you, it dies!'

The Doctor's mind was racing. 'Perhaps there's been some subterranean movement. That could account for it. Tell me, have you noticed any recent earth tremors?'

No one was interested in the Doctor's theories. A gong rang out, and a low chanting went up from the

Sisters. A beam of light shafted down from the chink high in the roof.

Ohica bowed low. 'It is time for the sacrifice, High One.'

Maren raised a withered hand. 'Take him. The Flame must be fed!'

Black-robed figures congregated around the Doctor, half carrying, half dragging him across the Temple. They took him to an area on the far side of the chamber, where there stood an upright pillar of stone, its sides sinisterly blackened. Faggots of wood were piled high around the pillar. The effect was that of one of Earth's November Fifth bonfires—and the Doctor was to be the Guy! He was thrust against the stone pillar and lashed to it. More sisters appeared, all bearing flaming torches. Desperately the Doctor yelled, 'Wait, Maren!'

The High Priestess hobbled across the Temple to stand before him. 'You had the chance of mercy, Doctor, and you refused it.'

'But this trouble you've been having could explain why I'm here. You may need scientific advice.'

The sound of the chanting drowned his voice. A Sister handed Maren a blazing torch, and she and the other Sisters began circling the Doctor's pyre in a kind of ritual dance.

The Doctor struggled frantically, but the cords were too strong. The dancing and chanting went on, and he wondered how much time he had left. He shouted again. 'This could be a grave mistake, Maren. If those gases have been sealed off, this whole mountain could go up ... Remember Popacatepetl!'

The dance went on, and the flaming torches came ever closer to the wood piled at the Doctor's feet. He wondered what would determine the final moment. Then he noticed the beam of sunlight. As the sun rose higher and higher, the shaft of light moved across the sanctum floor, coming nearer and nearer to the pile of faggots. The symbolism was clear. At the moment when the sunlight reached the pillar, the Sisters would thrust their flaming brands into the pyre, and the wood round the Doctor's feet would burst into roaring flame.

Struggling wildly against his bonds, the Doctor watched the beam of sunlight move slowly across the floor ...

5

Sarah to the Rescue

The weird chanting of the Sisters drifted faintly out of the cave mouth and across the mountainside. Solon gripped Condo's arm. 'That's the death song. The Song of Sacrifice!'

Condo looked baffled. 'They're making a Sacrifice to the Flame,' explained Solon impatiently. 'I have to see what's happening. We must get closer.'

Condo hung back. 'No, Master. Temple bad place. Evil spirits.'

Solon wasn't listening. 'A sacrifice to the Flame,' he muttered. 'They *never* offer one of their own. Always a stranger, an outsider. I have to *see* ...'

Solon began creeping towards the cave mouth. Condo hesitated, but his fear of Solon was even greater than his fear of the Sisters, and reluctantly he followed.

Sarah saw them go, from her hiding-place higher in the rocks. She watched them disappear inside the cave mouth. A moment or two later she climbed down the rocks and followed them inside.

Unaware of these new additions to the audience, the Doctor watched the torch-waving dancers move ever closer. The beam of sunlight was closer too, and clearly it would be only minutes before blazing torches were thrust into the piles of wood all round him. The dancers' eyes were glazed and they moved in a kind of self-induced trance. The Doctor realised it would be useless to try to reach them with appeals to reason. Grimly he went on struggling with his bonds, but the twine was strong and the knots held firm.

The ray of sunlight touched the bonfire. Maren stretched out her blazing torch, and the other Sisters did the same. The wooden faggots were already beginning to smoulder—when a shout of 'No!' rang loudly through the cavern.

The chanting stopped. The Sisters froze, like figures in some old painting. Maren turned slowly— to see Solon standing in the arched doorway, Condo looming behind him. 'No!' repeated Solon. 'You've got to stop!'

Maren hobbled slowly towards him. Her voice was icy cold as the snow on Karn's high mountains. 'What is the meaning of this?'

Solon shrank back. She was only a wizened old woman in a shabby black robe, but the force of her anger struck him like the heat of a furnace. He waved his hands in a clumsy gesture of apology. 'I am sorry, High One, deeply sorry.'

The terrible old voice said, 'It is death for out-siders to enter the Temple.'

The wailing voices of the Sisters took up the word. 'Death! Death! Death!' The chanting circle began to move closer to the two intruders. In blind panic, Condo snatched out his sword.

Maren raised her hand. Light flashed from an ornate ring on her finger, and Condo screamed with pain, dropping the sword and clutching his numbed shoulder. 'Bring them before me,' ordered Maren. The Sisters herded Solon and Condo across the Sanctum, and brought them to Maren where she stood by the Doctor's bound figure.

Unseen, another figure appeared in the arched doorway—Sarah. Quickly she took in the scene, the bound Doctor, the captive Solon and Condo. She paused for a moment and ran back into the antechamber, hunting round desperately. Her luck was in. A curtained alcove held a pile of black ceremonial robes. Sarah began struggling into one with desperate speed.

Meanwhile Solon stood before Maren, frantically trying to justify his intrusion. He was well aware that he was talking for his life. If the Sisters turned the full force of their psychic powers on him, they could blast the life from his body with their anger. 'Maren, High One,' he faltered. 'Believe me, I meant no harm ...'

'The harm is done. Already the sacrifice is defiled.'

'Might as well cancel the show then,' suggested a hopeful voice from inside the bonfire. 'Take no notice, Solon, *I'm* glad to see you!'

Ohica swung round. 'Be silent!'

'Didn't think much of the singing either,' continued the Doctor irrepressibly. 'What you need is a really good contralto.'

Ohica menaced him with her blazing torch. 'Enough! The High One commands you to silence!' The Doctor decided he'd better shut up, at least for the time being.

Solon seized his opportunity. 'Maren, I came only to ask a favour of the Sisters. I had no intention of offending——'

'What favour?'

Solon spread his hands ingratiatingly. 'In all the years since I came to Karn I have never asked anything of you until now. Indeed, in that time I have often helped you, treated your injuries.'

Maren made an impatient gesture. All this was true enough. Occasionally Solon *had* treated the Sisters for minor ailments and injuries. Although virtually immortal, they were as vulnerable to life's minor ailments as anyone else. But nothing Solon had done in the past could excuse the terrible blasphemy he had just committed. 'All this we know. What do you *want*, Solon?'

Solon pointed. 'The Doctor. I ask you to spare him.'

'Seconded!' called the cheery voice from the stake. 'Any against?' No one took any notice.

'The Doctor is condemned,' said Maren implacably. 'He must die in the Flame.'

'But High One, he is a Time Lord. Your long-standing alliance ...'

'... no longer exists!' snapped Maren.

Solon became desperate as he saw his long-awaited prize head slipping away. 'Maren, I beg you,' he cried. 'Let me have him, *please*!' He looked round wildly. 'If you must have a sacrifice—take my servant here.' He grabbed the reluctant Condo, thrusting him forward. Condo pulled himself free, growling angrily. He glared balefully at Solon.

Maren waved her hand in dismissal. '*Go*, Solon.

Leave *now*—while you still can.'

Solon fell to his knees, almost sobbing in desperation. 'Then if you *must* sacrifice him—let me have his head.'

Maren glared incredulously at him. 'His head?'

'Only as far as the cervical vertebrae. You can have the rest. But *please* don't destroy the head!' Solon gazed yearningly up at the Doctor. 'I need it, High One. I need it for ...'

Solon fell silent. He could tell no one why he needed the Doctor's head—particularly not the Sisterhood.

Maren had reached the end of her patience. 'We know of your unnatural experiments, Solon, and they hold no interest for us. We tolerate your presence here on Karn only as long as you keep your place. Because you have done us some small services in the past, I shall spare your life. But begone from here at once—or you too will die in the Flame!'

While Maren was speaking, the Doctor felt something sawing at his bonds. He glanced over his shoulder—and saw the face of Sarah beneath a black hood. The Doctor nodded urgently towards the doorway. Sarah nodded back her understanding. As the Doctor's bonds came free, she slipped back into the group of Sisters and began edging her way towards the door.

Solon bowed his head, accepting Maren's decision, and realising that he was lucky to leave the Sanctum alive. 'Yes, Maren—of course. I'm sorry, very sorry ...' Still mumbling apologies, Solon backed out of the chamber.

Maren ignored him. She raised her hand commandingly. 'Make the offering!'

'That's right, get on with it!' confirmed the Doctor. 'I've been ready for ages. It's very rude to keep the sacrifice hanging about!'

The ceremony moved to its climax. Maren chanted, 'Flame of Life, Fire of Death, take this intruder's body into thy eternal heart.'

The Sisters weaved closer, waving their burning torches. The ray of sunlight touched the edge of the bonfire, and they all plunged their torches into the wood. Specially treated with the highly flammable oil of rineweed, the wood burst into flame at a dozen points. The Doctor decided things were getting a little too hot for him. It was time to leave. He hurtled over the flames like a circus acrobat going through a blazing paper hoop, and his long legs had carried him clear across the Temple before the astonished Sisters had time to react. So fast was he moving that he shot straight past Sarah, who hadn't even reached the entrance.

Stripping off the encumbering robes, Sarah dashed after the Doctor. Maren was the first to recover her wits. She raised a hand and the ornate ring spat its ray of fire after the Doctor. But the Doctor was already through the arch and the fiery ray caught Sarah instead. She staggered a moment, her hands to her face, and stumbled blindly after the Doctor.

He was waiting on the other side of the arch. 'Come on, girl, come on! They'll be after us any minute.'

Sarah's hands were still clasped to her face. 'I can't, Doctor.'

The Doctor realised there was no time to ask what was wrong. He scooped Sarah off her feet, flung her over his shoulder, and started to run for both their lives.

With dragging footsteps Solon entered his hall and slumped down at the table by the fire. Chin in hands, he stared despondently into the ashes. 'What a *waste*! What a stupid, senseless *waste*.'

Condo came into the hall. He stood behind Solon, brooding over the seated figure. Suddenly he rumbled, 'You give Condo. Why?'

Solon ignored him.

The giant barbarian persisted, 'Condo *good* servant. Why give to Sisters? Why tell them kill Condo?'

Solon was so used to treating Condo as a kind of mindless automaton, he found it hard to realise that Condo had any feelings to be hurt. Irritably he snapped, 'Silence, you chattering ape, or I'll give you to them yet. Haven't I enough to think about without ...'

Condo's hook flashed out, gripping the material of Solon's robe and digging painfully into the flesh beneath. Solon was dragged to his feet. 'Condo kill you!' Already Condo's other hand had drawn the sword from his belt.

Solon struggled furiously. 'Don't be a fool, Condo!'

Condo gave a guttural laugh. 'You *try* to make Condo fool—but Condo *not* fool! Now *you* die!' With gloating slowness Condo raised the sword above his head.

Solon shrunk away from the gleaming blade. He struggled furiously, but the agonising pressure of the hook kept him held fast. A jumble of thoughts raced through Solon's mind. To die like this, with his great work unfinished. Worst of all to die at the hands, or rather hand and hook, of a nobody like Condo!

A babble of excuses and explanations poured from Solon's lips. 'Condo, what are you doing? Don't, for mercy's sake. I didn't *mean* it. I wouldn't have *let* them sacrifice you. It was a joke, that's all, a silly joke ...'

Condo frowned. 'You joke?'

Solon smiled weakly. 'That's right. Just a foolish joke.'

There was a pause while Condo's slow-thinking mind considered this new idea. Then he shook his head. 'You not joke. Condo not joke either. You lose head now!'

The sword flashed down. Solon flung himself back with a terrified scream, tearing his robe, and a pinch of his skin, free from the hook. He crashed to the ground, taking the table with him, rolled over and scrambled to his feet. Brandishing the sword, Condo advanced towards him. Solon backed away, clutching his wounded shoulder. 'Wait—Condo, wait ...' A saving thought flashed into Solon's mind. 'Your arm! You want your arm back, don't you? You can have it—if you let me live.'

Condo halted. 'Take off hook. Give back good arm and hand?'

Solon nodded eagerly. 'Would I lie to you? I *can* put your arm back, you know I can. It's what you always wanted, isn't it?'

Slowly Condo slid the sword back into his belt. 'Give arm now—Condo not kill.'

Solon gave a sigh of relief. The moment of revolt was over. It wouldn't take him long to re-establish his dominance over this stupid hulk. 'It will take a little time, Condo. There must be careful preparation. We can't have anything going wrong. You go and prepare the laboratory, and I'll go down to the preserving tanks and prepare the arm.'

Condo hesitated, then nodded and left the hall. Solon gasped with relief, mopping his brow with a many-coloured handkerchief. He followed Condo out of the hall, heading not up the stairs but down them. Here in the cellars of the castle were the tanks in which Solon kept those grisly remnants of living beings which were the subject of his experiments. Naturally there was no question of restoring Condo's arm. It had been put to far better use. In addition, Solon didn't want to lose his only hold over the giant servant. But he'd have to go through the motions of getting things ready. Later he could always find more reasons for delay. And if that didn't work—well, there were poisons in Solon's cabinet which would take care even of Condo.

At the foot of the steps was a heavy metal-studded door, leading into a kind of crypt. Solon moved quietly as he came near it. It was almost as if he was trying to creep unobserved. But his precautions were useless. From inside the crypt a deep groaning voice called, 'Solon! Come to me!'

Solon stopped, an expression of terror on his face.

The voice came again. It was a terrifying voice, thick with pain and hate. 'Solon!'

Solon moved to the door. Reluctantly he opened it, releasing a pulsating greenish glow which flickered eerily over his face. Slowly he moved inside the crypt ...

6

The Horror in the Crypt

The Doctor lowered Sarah carefully to the ground
under the shelter of an overhanging boulder, and
looked cautiously around. 'We seem to have given
the Sisters the slip. The barbecue is off, I'm happy to
say.'

Sarah was rubbing her eyes, moving her head to
and fro. 'Doctor,' she sobbed. 'I can't see.'

'What! Let me take a look.' The Doctor knelt
down beside her, turned her face into the light, and
peered into her eyes.

Sarah gazed sightlessly at him. 'I've gone blind. It
must have been that flash ...'

'Keep still,' muttered the Doctor. He went on
examining her eyes.

'How do they look?' asked Sarah anxiously.

'Perfectly normal,' said the Doctor briskly. He
straightened up. 'That flash must have numbed the
optic nerve. It'll probably wear off in a couple of
hours.'

'And if it doesn't? I suppose I can always sell
violets.' Sarah mimicked the traditional Cockney
whine. 'Luv'ly sweet vi'lets. Luv'ly vi'lets, Guvnor.'
She reverted to her normal tone. 'That's if we ever
get back to Piccadilly.'

The Doctor's face was full of concern, but he

allowed none of it to show in his voice. 'If you're going to sit there wallowing in self-pity, Sarah, I shall probably bite your nose.'

Despite herself, Sarah grinned at the childish threat. 'Typical. Thanks for the sympathy.'

The Doctor took her hands and lifted her to her feet. 'Come on ...'

'Where are we going?'

'Back to see Solon.'

Sarah pulled back. 'Oh no, we're not.'

The Doctor chuckled. 'Don't worry, Sarah, I've got the measure of old Solon now. Whatever else he is, he's a very gifted physician. He's obviously well acquainted with the Sisters. He may have some idea of the effect of their weapons and how to counter it.'

'He's a gifted maniac,' said Sarah vigorously. 'Do you know what he's got in that laboratory of his? A kind of monster body, no head, made out of lumps of this and that.' She poured out the story of her visit to Solon's laboratory, and of the horrible creature she had found behind the curtain.

The Doctor listened unsurprised. 'That's all very interesting, Sarah. But if my suspicions are correct, he's keeping something else alive in that Castle of his. Something far more dangerous than a mere headless monster! Come on, let's get started.'

Reluctantly, Sarah let the Doctor lead her across the rocky plain. Her fears were returning in full force. It was bad enough being suddenly blind. But to be blind on an alien planet full of unknown horrors ... And now the Doctor was leading them, by his own admission, straight towards the greatest danger of all ...

Solon stood in the doorway of the crypt, his face lit by the greenish glow from the centre of the room. 'I promise you faithfully that you will soon be free. I need just a little more time to conclude my experiments ...'

The deep voice was like a groan of pain. 'I grow weary of these endless promises, Solon. Always you need more time, more time!'

'If you could see how much has been accomplished, how little now remains to be done ...' A note of self-pity crept into Solon's voice. 'I have worked night and day in your service. When I first came here there was nothing. I had to build a laboratory out of ruined equipment, invent and construct my own apparatus before I could even begin my experiments.'

'Experiments!' said the voice scornfully. 'When we formed this plan to outwit the Time Lords, there was no talk of experiments. You told me that it could be done ...'

'And so it can,' said Solon passionately, 'so it can! I have made discoveries, mastered techniques no other man has even conceived. I can transplant limbs, organs, I can even create a life-form. All this against the most appalling difficulties ...'

'Yet I am still here,' the deep voice groaned. 'I can see nothing, feel nothing. I hear and speak only by means of your machines. You have locked me into hell for all eternity.'

'My lord, with so much at stake I cannot take *any* risks. Every step is an advance into totally new areas of medicine. Every step must be tested and tested again ...'

Angrily the voice boomed, 'Do you desire to be known as my creator rather than my servant?'

'No, no, my lord. You must trust me. I face so many problems. Even Condo has become unreliable. I shall probably have to put him down ...'

As if on cue, the voice of Condo echoed down the staircase, 'Master, Master, come quickly.'

'I must go. Forgive me, my lord.' As if he welcomed the interruption, Solon ducked out of the door. He was in such haste to leave that he left it ajar behind him.

'Come back, Solon, come back!'

Ignoring the summons, Solon ran back up the staircase.

Inside the hall, Condo stood waiting. Solon snarled, 'Well, what is it?'

Condo pointed. The Doctor and Sarah stood just inside the doorway. Solon reeled visibly with the shock. Then, steadying himself, he advanced on them with a welcoming smile. 'Doctor, how wonderful! What happened, did the Sisters release you after all?'

The Doctor shook his head. 'We left rather suddenly.'

'I did my best to save you, Doctor, even at the risk of my own life. You heard me plead with Maren. I tried to make them see reason ...'

'Yes, I noticed your concern. I was very touched.'

The Doctor spoke softly. But something in his expression made Solon profoundly uneasy. He licked his lips and tried another smile. 'Well, well, it's wonderful to see you again. Would you like some wine—' Solon broke off short, realising that this was rather a tactless offer, considering the circumstances in which they'd last drunk wine together.

The Doctor shook his head. 'No thank you, Solon, we've already had one taste of your hospitality. All I want from you is a professional opinion. I'd like you to examine Sarah's eyes.'

Solon looked baffled. 'I'm sorry, I don't follow ...'

'Sarah was blinded during our escape from the Sisters. I'd like you to examine her eyes.'

Solon looked calculatingly at the Doctor for a moment. Then he said smoothly. 'Yes, of course. I'll be glad to give any help I can. If you'll just come up to my laboratory ...' He gestured towards the stairs.

'After you,' said the Doctor politely. Solon set off, and the Doctor led Sarah after him.

Their search unsuccessful, the Sisters were filing back into the Temple. Ohica went across to Maren, and bowed low before her.

'We did not find them, High One. Yet they may still be hiding amongst the rocks. Shall I send out more searchers?'

Maren shook her head. 'The Time Lord cannot leave Karn.' She gestured towards the square blue shape of the TARDIS. 'We have his Space/Time machine. Sooner or later he will have to return for

70

it ... and we shall be ready for him.' There was a fierce glitter in Maren's eyes. 'Next time he will not be so fortunate, Ohica. When we capture him once more, he will wish that he had died in the Flame ...'

Unaware of the grisly plans being made for him, the Doctor stood by impatiently while Solon, an examining light clipped to his forehead, completed his examination of Sarah's eyes. 'Well?' the Doctor asked anxiously.

Solon was silent.

'Come on,' said Sarah, a little shakily. 'What's the verdict?'

'Oh, I think there's every chance, young lady. Yes, indeed, there's every chance of a full recovery. But I'll have to check my findings first, and work out a course of treatment.' Solon's voice was cheerful and confident, but there was a warning frown on his face as he looked at the Doctor. He turned back to Sarah. 'Meanwhile, my dear, perhaps you'd wait in the hall, while I talk to the Doctor?'

'Why?'

'Oh, medical etiquette, you know. We never discuss technicalities in front of the patient. Condo, would you take our young guest back to the hall for a moment?'

Sarah backed away, stumbling into the bench. 'No, Doctor, don't let him ...'

'It's all right, Sarah,' said the Doctor reassuringly. 'Condo's a changed man, now.' The Doctor's voice hardened. 'She'll be quite safe here—won't she, Solon?'

The threat in his voice was quite plain. Solon nodded eagerly. 'Of course. Condo, take good care of our guest. Serve her food, and something to drink.'

Condo's huge hand took Sarah's arm in a curiously gentle grip. 'Girl not see,' he rumbled. 'Condo help.'

Not much reassured, Sarah allowed herself to be led out of the room.

The Doctor waited until she was clear of the laboratory, then turned to Solon. 'Well?'

'I'm sorry, Doctor. Very sorry.'

'There's nothing you can do? You can't operate?'

Solon shook his head. 'I'm sorry. The retina is almost completely destroyed. There's nothing I can do for her ...'

'You're quite sure?' persisted the Doctor. 'Nothing at all?'

Solon sighed artistically. 'Not unless—but no, it's impossible. No one could be expected to ...'

'Not unless *what*?'

Solon took off his examining light and threw it on the bench. 'The Elixir of Life, Doctor. The mysterious substance the Sisters distill from their Sacred Flame. As you know, it assists tissue regeneration. But there's no hope of ...'

The Doctor moved towards the door. 'If that's what's needed, then that's what I'll get.'

Solon frowned. 'But how, Doctor? The Sisters control the only source. They'll kill you if you go back to the Temple.'

The Doctor shrugged. 'If I go back voluntarily, they'll have to give me a hearing.'

'You don't know the Sisterhood ...'

But the Doctor was already on his way. He paused at the door. 'It would be too dangerous to take Sarah with me. I'm leaving her here in your care. I advise you to guard her life as you would your own. Do I make myself clear?'

There was no mistaking the menace in the Doctor's voice. Something about his tone made Solon shiver. But his voice was level as he replied. 'There's no need to concern yourself, Doctor. Your young friend will be quite safe.'

'She'd better be,' said the Doctor grimly, and disappeared from the room.

Solon watched him go, a faint smile on his face. He gave himself a mental pat on the back. He'd handled the situation very well. Just enough attempts at dissuasion to be convincing, but not enough to stop the Doctor from going. Oh, he'd been suspicious, of course. But then, what alternative did he have? He *had* to go back to the Temple. Congratulating himself on his own brilliance, Solon crossed to a cluttered bench, found pen and paper and began to write.

In the hall, the Doctor was saying a hasty farewell to Sarah. 'I've *got* to leave you here for a bit, but with any luck it won't be long. Solon's pretty confident of a complete cure but there's a missing ingredient I've got to get for him. I've put the fear of the Time Lords into him, so don't worry.' Snatching up his now dried hat and scarf, the Doctor was gone before Sarah could protest.

Condo came back with a loaded tray. He led Sarah to a table, sat her down before it. He guided her hands to the table. 'Here. Biscuit. Cheese. Milk. Girl eat.'

The biscuit was dry, the cheese rank, and the milk decidedly peculiar. But at least it was a breakfast of a kind, and Sarah did her best to eat something. Condo stood watching her, his fierce face a little less harsh than usual. A voice rang down the stairway. 'Condo!'

Condo grunted. 'Master call. Condo go to him.'

Sarah heard him going up the stairs. Realising she was alone in the hall, she had a moment of panic. Even Condo was better than no one. Then willing herself to stay calm, she went on with her meal.

As Condo entered the laboratory, Solon was folding and sealing his letter. 'Condo, I want you to take this to the Sisters, do you understand?'

Condo shook his head. 'No! Condo not go to Sisters. They kill him.'

'Don't worry, you'll be in no danger. Just give them the letter, that's all.'

'What about arm? Solon promise to give back good arm and hand.'

'I'm working on it now, Condo. But unless I help the Doctor, he'll destroy me. Then you'll never get your arm back. Please, Condo, this one last favour. Then you'll have your arm back, I swear it!'

Condo took the letter.

'Now *hurry*,' said Solon eagerly. 'Whatever happens you must get to the Sisters before the Doctor. Take the short cut through the gorge. Oh, and leave by the back way, Condo, the girl mustn't know you've gone!'

Condo nodded, took the letter and left the laboratory.

Faintly in the distance. Sarah heard a deep groaning voice. 'Solon ... Solon ... Where are you?'

There was such pain and anguish in the voice that Sarah felt she *had* to respond. Uncertainly she stood up, and took a few paces towards the sound. 'Hello!' she called. 'Who is it? Who's there?'

The low moan floated towards her. 'Solon, is that you? Come to me, Solon.'

It was obvious that whoever was calling out was in great pain and distress. There was a compelling, hypnotic note in the voice, and despite her blindness Sarah felt she had to try and help. She tried to summon up a picture of the hall in her mind. There was the main door, the fireplace, the table where she'd been eating. At the back of the hall there had been stairs, leading both up and down. It was from that direction that the sound seemed to be coming.

Arms outstretched like a sleepwalker, Sarah moved slowly towards the stairs. There were odd tables and chairs scattered about, and several times she stumbled against them. But at last her outstretched fingertips touched a large rounded pillar—the central column of the great stone staircase. All this time the voice had continued. 'Solon ... where are you, Solon?' It was much nearer now, and there was no doubt as to the direction. It was coming from below.

Cautiously, step by step, Sarah began descending the staircase, holding on to the central pillar for support. With every step the summoning voice became louder and clearer.

The steps ended and she was standing on level flagstones again. There was a rough stone wall beside her, and she felt her way along it until she came to a space—an open door.

The voice was very loud now. It held anger as well as pain, and it was coming from inside the door. 'Solon? Have you come at last?'

Sarah groped her way inside the room. 'Who is it? What's the matter?'

There was an astonished silence. Slowly the voice said, *'Who are you?'*

'Just a visitor. I wondered if I could help. Is something wrong? Are you ill? I'm afraid I can't do much, I can't see. But I'll wait with you until Solon comes ...'

The response was a howl of anger. 'Where have you come from? Are you one of the Sisterhood? Did that hag Maren send you to destroy me?'

Sarah shrank back terrified. The voice seemed quite mad, beyond the reach of reason. Weakly she said, 'No, of course not. I came to help.'

'You lie!' screamed the voice. 'You came to kill me. You she-devils want to destroy me before I can wreak my vengeance on you!'

Sarah peered blindly towards the voice, wondering if she was trapped with a madman. And so indeed she was, in a way ... though with one that had, for the moment, no power to harm her.

Sarah wished desperately that she could see. But perhaps at this moment, her blindness was something of a blessing. The anguished threatening voice that so

terrified her came from a greenly-glowing tank in the
centre of the room. The tank was filled with nutrient
fluids. In its centre floated a spongy grey and purple
mass ... the still-living brain of Morbius.

7

Solon's Trap

Although Sarah, of course, couldn't see them, delicate electronic connections ran from the brain to instruments in the side of the tank. Solon's scientific genius had preserved Morbius in a kind of ghastly pseudo-life. Nutrients in the tank kept the brain alive. Complex electronic circuitry enabled the brain to hear and converted its electric impulses into speech. But the brain could not see, and it could not feel. The whole of physical life, touch, taste, sight, smell, awareness of light, heat, cold ... all these were gone.

On the Earth in Sarah's time, scientists had conducted experiments into something called 'sensory deprivation'. Subjects had floated in a tank of warm fluid, wearing suits and helmets that cut off all sensation. They could see nothing, hear nothing, feel nothing. Deprived of 'input' of all the millions of signals we constantly receive from the world about us, the subjects had begun to have hallucinations, to lose all sense of time and place, and eventually to go mad.

Something like this was happening to Morbius. Thanks to Solon's electronic devices he *was* able to hear and speak. But the loss of all other sensory functions, of all his physical being, was beginning to upset the balance of his mind. The waiting time in this limbo of non-existence had gone on too long, and Morbius was now perilously close to madness.

This very thought was occupying Solon's mind, as he hurried down the stairs towards the crypt. Even if he did eventually succeed in providing the brain of Morbius with a physical body—would the creature that resulted be the once great leader he had revered? Or would he have created an insane monster?

His thoughts were interrupted by voices from inside the door of the crypt. 'Honestly,' Sarah was saying. 'I really don't know what you're *talking* about . . .'

Solon flung open the door in a rage. 'You! What are you doing down here, girl?'

By now Sarah was so frightened that she was almost glad of Solon's arrival. 'I heard this voice,' she stammered. 'I only came down to see if I could help.'

'Nobody is allowed down here. *Nobody!*' shrieked Solon. 'You could have done untold damage to my most delicate equipment. Now, get out . . .'

He grabbed Sarah and dragged her to the door. The voice from the tank boomed, 'Solon!' Solon gave Sarah a final shove that sent her staggering into the corridor. He turned to face his master, moving nearer to the tank.

Sarah heard the voice say, 'Solon, you have lied to me!'

Then Solon's quick denial. 'Lied? I have never lied to you, my lord Morbius.'

Sarah gasped. 'Morbius!' Somehow he was alive, and in that room. She crept nearer to the door.

Morbius said angrily, 'You told me we were alone here.'

'The Doctor and the girl returned but a short time ago. If you could see the Doctor's head, Morbius! It is *perfect* for our purpose. As soon as I have it, I shall begin the final operation.'

'If the head is suitable, Solon, why have you not already taken it?'

'This Doctor is cunning. Already he suspects me. He knows of my past history, Morbius—and of yours!'

'You have your servant, do you not? This Condo? Did you not tell me his strength was that of a giant?'

Solon was horrified. 'I dare not use brute force, my lord. If there were to be a struggle, the head might suffer some injury. It must be in perfect condition, to house such a brain as yours.'

'Do you think I care for that? Just to walk again, to feel, to see ...'

'Naturally that is how you think now, my lord ...' said Solon nervously. 'But when you are a physical entity once again, imagine how you will see yourself, how important your new form will be to you.'

Morbius groaned. 'Solon, I think of nothing else. Trapped like this, like a sponge decaying in some murky sea ... no, even a sponge has more life than I do.' There was both agony and self pity in the deep voice. 'I, Morbius, who once dominated the High Council of the Time Lords, reduced to a condition where I envy a vegetable.'

'I beg you, Morbius, endure for only a little longer. I have sent the Doctor into a trap ...'

Outside in the corridor, Sarah tensed. She heard Solon go on, 'He has returned to visit the shrine of the Sisterhood—but they are warned and waiting.

Before the day is over he will be dead. In return for delivering him into their hands, I have asked only that the Sisters give me his head ...'

Sarah had been listening with increasing anger to this grisly conversation. Solon's gloating claim to have betrayed the Doctor was too much to be borne. With a sudden burst of energy she slammed the iron door. Her groping fingers found the keyhole with its huge iron key, and she locked the door.

Solon spun round as the door slammed shut and the key turned. Furiously he hurled himself upon it, pounding with his fists. 'Open it! Open this door, d'you hear me? You'll die for this!'

Morbius, helplessly suspended in his tank, called out, 'What has happened, Solon?'

Angrily Solon turned. 'The girl has locked me in here. A senseless gesture!'

The same thought was in Sarah's mind as she felt her way back up the staircase. Behind her she could hear Solon's muffled voice. 'When Condo returns, you shall die! You're wasting your time with this stupidity!'

He was probably quite right, thought Sarah gloomily. After all, what could she do, blind and helpless? But to look at it another way, it was pretty clear what she *couldn't* do. She couldn't stay in the castle, waiting meekly to be found and killed. And she couldn't let the Doctor walk into a trap without making some attempt, however futile, to find him and warn him of his danger.

Sarah felt her way carefully across the hall and towards the front door. She did much better on this

6

second journey, and encouraged by her success she managed to find the door and open it.

She stood on the threshold for a moment, welcoming the cool air on her face, trying to gather her courage. She had never felt so helpless and so alone. Her only hope was that the Doctor would somehow escape Solon's trap, and find her on his return to the castle. It was a slender hope, but Sarah clung to it, since it was all she had. She tried to summon up a picture of the approach to the castle, the path, the drawbridge and the rocky plains. Cautiously she started to move forwards.

In the Temple, the Ceremony of the Flame was reaching its end. This was the most sacred of all the rites of the Sisterhood. The Elixir of Life, drawn from the living flame, was ceremonially administered to the Sisters one by one. Its mystic powers arrested the ageing process, preserving them at the age at which they had joined the order. In its full form the ceremony was an impressive sight, with the entire Temple filled with row upon row of chanting black-robed sisters. But this particular ceremony was sadly reduced in size. Only a handful of Sisters passed before Maren, kneeling in turn to sip the Elixir from the silver chalice. The great bronzed screens were drawn back, and the sacred Flame leaped high, burning with a brilliance that only Maren and Ohica knew to be false.

Maren chanted. 'From the Sacred Flame you have been granted the precious gift of life eternal. Cherish and serve the Flame forever, my Sisters.'

The last of the Sisters sipped the precious Elixir, bowed low, and left the Temple. Only Maren and Ohica were left before the Flame, which was beginning to burn low. Maren gestured towards it. 'Now our Sisterhood is doomed, Ohica. That was the last of the Ceremonies of the Flame. You and those others who attended it will survive longest—at last you too shall perish, as I will.'

'You mean ... there is no more Elixir?'

'That was the last ... and the Flame is too low now to give us more.'

Ohica stared into the dying Flame. It was a symbol of her life, of all their lives. When it died, she and her Sisters would die also. For the Elixir of the Flame had to be regularly consumed to have its effect. Once begun, the treatment had to be continued. If not, the ageing process, so long held back, occurred with horrifying rapidity. The worst punishment for offending Sisters was that the Elixir should be withheld. Ohica remembered one such offender, long years ago, banished from the order for betraying its secrets to the followers of Morbius. After her expulsion she had forced her way into the ceremony, begging to be taken back, to receive the life-giving Elixir once more. Maren had refused—and before their eyes the offending Sister had withered into an ancient crone, collapsing in a heap of dusty bones. And now the same fate awaited them all.

'But, High One, you yourself should have been among those who drank of the Elixir. It is your right.'

Maren shook her head. 'There was only enough

Elixir for a handful of our Sisters. Besides, what use to postpone my fate?'

Ohica looked sadly at her High Priestess. Maren was already old. The weight of all her years would fall on her with horrifying suddenness. Sadly Ohica whispered, 'You know what will happen, Maren? To you, and to us all?'

Maren bowed her head. 'It is ordained. It is useless to defy one's fate.'

A Sister entered, carrying a letter. 'A message, High One, brought by Solon's servant.'

Maren frowned and took the letter. 'What did he say?'

'Nothing, High One. He thrust the note upon a Sister at the cave mouth and then fled.'

Maren smiled grimly, unfolded the note and read it. She passed it to Ohica. 'It seems the Doctor is returning to us.'

'Already? Why, High One?'

'Read for yourself. Solon claims to have tricked him, to have delivered him into our hands.'

Ohica studied the letter. 'And in return he asks that we slay the Doctor, preserve the head undamaged and return it to him. Insolent fool, does he seek to bargain with *us*?'

'The Doctor too is insolent, Ohica. Yet he is no fool. Has he no fear of our Sisterhood? Does he think that death—*his* death—is a trivial thing, a subject for jest. You remember how even bound to the sacrificial stake he mocked us!'

Ohica remembered very clearly. There had been something about the Doctor's gaiety and vigour that had impressed her deeply. She remembered his laughter. It had been a long time since anyone had laughed in the musty caverns where the Sisterhood made their home. She handed Solon's letter back to Maren. 'What shall we do?'

Maren crumpled the parchment. 'We shall show the Doctor that the Sisterhood still has the strength to destroy intruders. Alert the guards, Ohica. This time the Doctor shall not escape alive!'

Ohica hesitated. It seemed almost as if she was about to speak, perhaps even to object—though to disobey an order of the High One was unthinkable.

Maren snapped, 'Go, Ohica!'

Ohica left the Sanctum.

Sarah stumbled over an unseen rock, her foot twisted, and she fell heavily. She lay still for a moment, almost worn out. It wasn't her first fall on this nightmare journey, and she knew it wouldn't be her last. Considering that she was attempting to cross a stretch of mountainous, largely unknown country in the equivalent of pitch darkness, she was lucky not to have fallen over some precipice by now.

She picked herself up and stumbled on, hands stretched out before her. Before long she touched a rough stone surface—she guessed it was the side of one of the huge boulders that littered the plain.

She was just beginning to work her way round it, when she heard heavy footsteps pounding towards her. Instinctively Sarah dropped to the ground, huddling under the boulder for shelter.

She heard the footsteps come closer, and soon she could hear the deep sobbing breath of the unseen runner. Sarah lay as still as a rabbit trying to escape a fox. She knew the footsteps weren't those of the Doctor. She thought that the terrified runner sounded like Condo, and she had no wish to run into *him* again.

Sarah heard the footsteps come closer, closer— then blunder on past and disappear into the distance. She waited a little longer, then, struggling to her feet, she resumed her seemingly endless, hopeless journey.

At about this time the Doctor was nearing the cave that led into the Sisterhood's Temple. He found himself a position on a rock ledge overlooking the cave and waited for some time. He hoped to find some wandering Sister who could take a message in to Maren, asking for a meeting. But the area seemed deserted—the Sisterhood had gone to ground. The Doctor considered looking for an alternative entrance. But it occurred to him that the more secretive his approach the more easily would the suspicions of the Sisters be aroused. 'March up to the front door and ring the bell, that's the thing,' he told himself. Getting to his feet, the Doctor climbed boldly down the rocks and approached the entrance to the cave.

The cave mouth, and the tunnel beyond it, loomed darkly before him. In the distance the Doctor could see the flickering of a wall torch. 'Well, they must be about somewhere,' he thought. 'Unless they've gone out and left the lights on.' He went into the cave and made his way down the tunnel.

He walked slowly and carefully, expecting to be challenged at any moment. Nothing happened. At last the ante-chamber came in sight. Beyond that, the Doctor knew, was the Temple itself. He paused, waiting. Still nothing. 'Ding, dong!' said the Doctor loudly. There was no reply. He took a few paces forward—and a weighted net dropped from the roof, swaddling him in its web. Sisters ran from the ante-chamber, and pulled the net tight about him, trapping his arms and legs. More Sisters appeared, carrying long sharp tridents, holding their points close to his body.

The Doctor made no attempt to resist, watching these warlike proceedings with an air of quiet amusement, like a kindly uncle at a children's party. He looked round the circle of fiercely glaring Sisters and smiled. 'My dear young ladies,' he said reprovingly. 'We really can't go on meeting like this!'

As always with the Sisterhood, the Doctor's little joke failed to raise even a smile. Jabbing tridents urged him forwards, and stumbling a little in the folds of the net, he was taken across the ante-chamber and into the Temple.

8

The Doctor Makes a Bargain

Condo bounded swiftly across the rocks, intent on reaching the safety of the castle. In his panic-stricken hurry he failed to notice the huddled shape of Sarah beneath a nearby boulder. He had always regarded the Sisterhood with superstitious awe and terror, and it had taken all his courage just to hand over Solon's letter.

At last the drawbridge came in sight, and Condo hurtled across it, flung open the door, and collapsed panting inside the empty hall. He looked round in puzzlement. The girl had gone. Perhaps Solon had already killed her. Condo felt an unaccustomed pang of regret. Something about Sarah's helplessness had touched a long buried streak of tenderness in him. Somehow he didn't like to think of Sarah's head in one of Solon's preserving jars.

Slowly he made his way up to the laboratory. But that too was empty—except for the thing behind the curtains of the bed. Condo had never seen it, and had no wish to. Solon had forbidden him even to look at his creation. Condo came down the stairs into the hall again, and stood puzzled for a moment. He heard muffled sounds of shouting and pounding from somewhere below. He crossed to the stairs and called, 'Master? Master?'

Faintly Solon's voice came back. 'Down here, Condo. Hurry!'

Condo ran down the stairs and tried the door of the crypt. It wouldn't move. 'Door not open, Master,' he called.

'That's because it's locked, you great oaf,' said Solon's angry voice.

Condo turned the key and opened the door. Solon shot out of the crypt, slamming the door on the protesting voice behind him. Faithful disciple as he was, Solon felt he couldn't endure another second of Morbius's nagging reproaches.

Condo stared at him. 'Why Master locked inside?'

'The girl, you fool. *She* locked me in.' He shoved Condo towards the stairs. 'Go and find her, Condo. She can't have got far. Bring her back here. I've a score to settle with that young lady!'

The atmosphere in the gloomy-shadowed Temple was tense. Free of the net, but still surrounded by the three-pointed spears of his guards, the Doctor stood before Maren, who glared malevolently down from her throne. 'Why have you returned?'

'I think I need some of that Elixir of yours.'

'Indeed, Doctor? So at last you confess—you *did* come to steal the Elixir.'

'I don't want it for myself—*or* for the Time Lords,' said the Doctor impatiently. 'As a matter of fact, it's your fault I need the stuff at all. Sarah was blinded by a ray from your ring. I'm told I need the Elixir to restore her sight.'

'Solon told you this?'

The Doctor nodded. 'That's right.'

'Strange, Doctor. Solon knows full well that the effect of the ray lasts but a short time. It stuns the optic nerves, not destroys them. The girl will soon recover.'

'Unnecessary journey, eh? Well, I had my suspicions, I must admit. Never mind, I wanted to have a chat with you anyway.'

'You are rash, Doctor. Have you forgotten that we have condemned you to die?'

The Doctor snorted impatiently. 'Oh really, we're not going through all that business again, are we? If I really intended to steal from you, I'd scarcely walk in through the front door, now would I?'

'Then why have you come? Why did you come to Karn at all, if not to steal?'

'Not of my own accord, I assure you. I rather fancy I *was* sent by the Time Lords—but I won't be able to tell you why until I know what Solon is up to.'

'Solon cares only for his foul experiments on the bodies of the dead.'

'Experiments, yes—but to what purpose? Why was he so keen on getting his hands on my head? I must know what Solon intends ... I have the feeling that something incredibly evil is brewing.'

'If that was so, we should know of it.' It was Ohica who spoke. 'Nothing happens on Karn without our knowledge.'

'A Time Lord could live here without your knowledge. He could place a barrier around his mind.'

Maren leaned forward on her throne. 'What are you suggesting?'

'Morbius was a Time Lord.'

There was a moment of silence. Then Maren rose to her feet. 'That name again! I tell you Morbius is dead. I *saw* his execution. I *saw* the body placed in the dispersal chamber. Nothing of Morbius, not the smallest atom, exists!'

The Doctor frowned. It was clear that Maren believed what she was saying—and yet ... The Doctor remembered the sudden impression of mind-contact just as he was losing consciousness under Solon's drugged wine. 'Was Solon living on Karn at that time?'

Maren gestured dismissively. 'Who knows? There were many on Karn, then. They came from all over the galaxy to attend the trial of Morbius.'

The Doctor stood lost in thought. He remembered the story well, though he himself had taken no part in it. Still a fugitive from his own people he had been roaming distant galaxies in his TARDIS, swearing to have no further part in the concerns of the Time Lords. The Doctor smiled ironically, remembering how things had turned out.

But in those days ... even in the remotest parts of the Universe, rumours had reached him. Morbius, greatest of the High Council of the Time Lords, had sought to lead his people into paths of domination and conquest. Rejected by his people, he had fled from them in rage and anger. He had gone from planet to planet, preaching his gospel of conquest and destruction, raising an army of followers, leaving chaos and destruction behind him. Finally the Time Lords had rallied. They too had raised an army, an alliance of all the civilised life-forms menaced by Morbius and his hordes. They had hunted him through the galaxy, cornered him here on Karn, defeated him in one last terrible battle that had left the planet in ruins. Shaken out of their usual complacency by the revolt, the Time Lords had acted swiftly for once. Morbius had been tried and executed immediately, on the planet that was the scene of his final defeat.

Musingly the Doctor said, 'Morbius was a war criminal, right enough. A ruthless dictator who wanted to rule the entire galaxy. But even in defeat, he had millions of fanatical followers and admirers.'

'Riff-raff,' said Maren contemptuously. 'Mercenaries! The army he brought to Karn was the scum of the galaxy.'

Ohica took up the story. 'And why did he bring them here? Why choose Karn? Because he had promised his followers immortality. He promised them the Elixir of Life!'

Maren spoke broodingly. 'Morbius betrayed our secret. Since then we must remain constantly on guard against the entire cosmos. Yet we can still defend ourselves!'

'Yes, and that's another thing,' said the Doctor sternly. 'You really can't go on dragging innocent travellers to their deaths, wrecking their spaceships with telekinetic energy.'

'Innocent?' snapped Maren. 'They come to steal.

'Some perhaps,' agreed the Doctor. 'Others might

just be passing by, as I was. No, if I'm going to help you, there must be no more indiscriminate destruction of spaceships. Is it a bargain?'

For a moment Maren was struck speechless by the Doctor's audacity. She had ruled for so long that she was unable to take in the idea that someone was giving *her* orders. Furiously she said, 'Your insolence is limitless, Doctor. I have only to raise a finger and you will be put to death.'

The Doctor shrugged. 'No doubt. But I'd be very little use to you dead, Maren. And you do have a problem.' He nodded towards the alcove, where the great bronze shields were once more in place. 'No Flame, no Elixir. Pretty soon, no Sisterhood.'

'When the Flame dies, the Sisterhood dies. So it is ordained,' said Ohica sadly.

'Rubbish! The Flame is a natural phenomenon, despite all the mumbo-jumbo you ladies have built up over the years. There's nothing mystical about it. If the Flame *is* dying there's a reason, a natural scientific, physical reason.'

'Blasphemer!' shrieked Maren. 'I have served the Flame for centuries and I *know*. There is nothing to be done.'

The Doctor spread his hands. 'Then there's no harm in letting me try—is there?'

'He is right, Maren. Let him try to help us!'

Maren turned in astonishment, and Ohica quailed beneath the High Priestess's angry glare. Her voice trembled, but she forced herself to go on. 'I mean no offence, High One. But I say again. *Let him try.* Where is the harm?'

Maren brooded for a long time. It was hard for her to change ideas that had crystallised over so many centuries. But if there was any hope that the Sisterhood could be saved ... She gestured abruptly, 'Let the guards retire to the outer chamber.'

The spear-carrying Sisters silently withdrew. Maren hobbled over to the alcove, and threw back the bronze gates. 'You are privileged, Doctor. No eyes outside our order are permitted to look upon the Flame of Life.'

The Doctor saw that the Flame was indeed very low. Flickering and weak, it was no more than a few inches high. He peered at it. 'Is it always this reddish colour?'

'Always.'

'Fascinating.' The Doctor leaned over the flame till he was in danger of singeing the end of his nose. 'Presumably the heat of the Flame causes oxidisation of the minerals in the rock ... there's a chemical reaction with rising super-heated gases from deep in the heart of the planet ... and your Elixir forms in here.' The Doctor straightened up, tapping the silver chalice set into the bowl of rock. 'Incredible! The impossible dream of a thousand alchemists, dripping like tea from an urn.'

Maren shook her head impatiently at the Doctor's flood of scientific speculation. 'Do not try to understand, Doctor,' she intoned solemnly. 'These are mysteries beyond the reach of the mind.'

The Doctor smiled. 'I doubt they're beyond the reach of a decent spectograph, my dear Maren. One could probably analyse your Elixir and reproduce it by the gallon, but the consequences would be catastrophic. That's why the Time Lords have always helped you to keep your precious secret.'

Maren shook her head disgustedly, but Ohica was intrigued. 'What do you mean, Doctor? Why catastrophic?'

'Everyone wanting to live for ever?' The Doctor shook his head. 'It would lead to universal stagnation. Death is the price we pay for progress.'

Maren was stung into a reply. 'You speak in riddles, Doctor, like all your race. You Time Lords were glad enough of our Elixir—and glad enough to keep it to yourselves.'

The Doctor sighed. 'We use the Elixir, true, Maren. But we don't depend on it. It's a useful medicine, where there's some difficulty in body regeneration. But we don't take it regularly as you do—otherwise we'd fall into the same trap.'

'Trap?' demanded Maren indignantly. 'And what trap have we fallen into, Doctor?'

'Immortality,' said the Doctor simply. 'We Time Lords live long, and we live many lives. But we are *not* immortal, Maren, nor do we wish to be. With us bodily regeneration is a natural process. In time it comes to an end, and we die, as do all living things.' The Doctor looked sympathetically at Maren's wizened form. 'You were old when the Elixir was discovered, Maren. How many centuries have passed while you lived in these caves unchanged? How long since *anything* here has changed?' His voice hardened. 'You think you have eternal life? Look around you. You have condemned yourself to eternal death!'

Ohica whispered. 'It is true, Doctor. Nothing here ever changes.'

The Doctor felt a little ashamed of his sudden outburst. 'Precisely my point, my dear. No progress, you see!' He started groping in his capacious pockets. 'Now let me see. As I remember I spent last November the Fifth on the planet Earth. They have a kind of Ceremony of the Flame themselves, you know.'

Ohica looked on in astonishment as the Doctor produced a stubby cylinder from his pocket. It was wrapped in brightly coloured paper and there was a twist of dark-blue paper at one end. The Doctor beamed. 'Now then, ladies, I advise you to stand well back!'

Ohica stared at him. 'What is that, Doctor?'

The Doctor read the writing on the side of the cylinder. 'They call it a Little Demon.' He touched the blue paper to the tiny Flame, and as it began to smoulder, he forced it through the crevice from which the Flame issued.

Maren ran forward in horror. 'Stop! No one has ever touched the sacred Flame ...'

There was a sudden pop, and the Flame went out.

'The Flame is dead!' gasped Ohica.

Maren looked appalled, then sprang into furious life. 'Guards, take him,' she screamed. Spear-carrying Sisters ran back into the chamber. In an instant the needle-sharp points were at the Doctor's throat. 'You have defiled the secret of the Flame.' hissed Maren. 'Now your blood shall wet the sacred rocks to mourn its passing! Kill him!' The spears came closer, the Doctor backed towards the alcove ... There was a sudden roar, a gush of smoke and the Flame spurted high in the fountain, higher than ever before. The awe-stricken guards drew back. Maren and Ohica fell to their knees.

'Soot,' said the Doctor, happily regarding the leaping fountain of the Flame. 'Centuries of corrosion, you see. There'll be no charge—but I *would* like a little help with my problems now.'

Maren rose to her feet, and waved the trembling guards away. 'Of course,' continued the Doctor chattily, 'it will be quite a while before you get more Elixir. The rock has to warm right through.'

Maren hobbled back to her throne and stared almost angrily down at the Doctor. 'So now you expect us to show our gratitude? Is that it, Doctor?'

The Doctor looked thoughtfully at her. 'Well ...' he said deprecatingly. As a matter of fact, the Doctor wasn't sure what he expected. True he had solved Maren's problem. But he had forced the solution on her in a way that challenged her most precious beliefs. It wasn't hard for him to guess what was in Maren's mind. If she killed him now, no one need ever know that she had been forced to accept his help. Everything could go on as it had for so many centuries. To one of Maren's autocratic temperament, the temptation must be a strong one. Would she order the Sisterhood to help him—or kill him?

Calmly the Doctor waited for Maren's decision.

9

The Monster Walks

Sarah must have stumbled blindly across the rocky plains for most of the day. Hunger and thirst made her delirious, and she lost all sense of time. Finally, too weary even to crawl, she collapsed into an exhausted sleep.

When she awoke it had become much colder, and Sarah guessed the sun must be going down. It would soon be night. One good thing about being blind, she reflected bitterly, you were no worse off when it got dark. Except, she suddenly realised, it made her chances of being found by the Doctor even slimmer. Wearily Sarah started getting to her feet. There seemed no point in going on—but it was better than freezing to death on the spot. Maybe she'd survive a few hours longer if she kept moving. She put a hand out to steady herself and touched something smooth and rounded. Not rock, but leather or plastic ... with a thrill of horror Sarah realised she was touching the toe-cap of an enormous boot. A giant hand clamped round her wrist and dragged her to her feet. She stretched her other hand out before her and touched—what? An arm? It seemed to be made of some hard unyielding material—and ended not in a hand but a steel hook! Sarah had been found at last. But not by the Doctor. By Condo.

She began struggling wildly. 'Please, let me go. I've got to find the Doctor.'

The deep voice growled, 'No. Girl come. Master send Condo find girl.'

'Why—What does he want me for?'

'Master very angry. Maybe kill!'

Sarah remembered locking Solon in the crypt. Clearly he was taking it badly. She tried to pull away. 'No, let me go, please.'

'Master say find girl—Condo obey! But Condo not kill. Girl pretty. Condo like.'

Sarah paused. The thought of making an ally of this murderous barbarian was something that simply hadn't occurred to her. But she could certainly do with a friend. 'Well if you'd stop breaking my arm, I might like you a bit better.'

There was sadness in the deep voice. 'Girl not like Condo. Condo ugly. Girl afraid.'

Sarah said coaxingly. 'Nonsense, Condo. Look, *please* let me go, I need to find the Doctor.'

'Doctor dead. Solon trick him. Betray to Sisters—Sisters kill!'

'No, you're lying. He isn't dead, he can't be.'

'Doctor dead. Better you come now. Master want.'

Ignoring Sarah's protests, Condo slung her over his shoulder like a sack and bounded back towards the castle.

Some time later after a very bumpy journey, Condo carried Sarah into the hall, up the stairs and dumped her down in a chair in Solon's laboratory. She heard Solon's angry voice. 'Condo, you fool—at last! Why did it take you so long to find one blind girl?'

'Girl travel far—brave.' said Condo defensively. 'Master not hurt girl.'

'Why I've misjudged you,' sneered Solon. 'Under that brutish exterior there's a tender, compassionate nature.'

'Condo *like* girl.' There was a note of dangerous obstinacy in the deep voice. 'Master not hurt.'

'Dear me, he's *such* a romantic.'

Realising Solon was addressing her, Sarah muttered weakly, 'You think you're a bundle of laughs, don't you?' It wasn't much of a come-back but she was too exhausted to manage anything in the way of sparkling repartee.

Sarah felt Condo's big hand touch her hair. 'Hair pretty.'

Solon lost patience. 'All right, Condo, that's enough drooling for now. You'd better get her some food and drink if you're so worried about her. From the looks of her she'll probably die on us if we don't feed her.'

Sarah heard Condo's footsteps move away. She felt Solon fastening her to the chair with heavy straps. 'Must make sure our guest doesn't leave us again ...' She heard him chuckle, and his hand stroked her hair, mimicking Condo's gesture. 'Poor Condo. Perhaps I'll let him have your hair as a souvenir. Better still, I'll give him the whole head!'

'You're insane, Solon, you know that? You're raving mad!'

She heard Solon's angry gasp. 'Oh, no, that's what they all said—but it was jealousy! They envied my achievements!'

Sarah realised she had touched a nerve. This wasn't

the first time Solon had been accused of insanity, and he was very sensitive on the subject. The angry voice ranted on. 'When I said I could sustain life in the organs of the dead, they mocked me. Only Morbius had the faith to believe in me. Only Morbius! I bribed the guards, so I was able to steal his brain *before* they destroyed his body. I kept it alive!' She heard him pace across the room and there was a swish of curtains. Solon must be looking at the ghastly creation on the bed. 'One day soon they'll all choke on their laughter. I made *this*! Every part is functioning perfectly, exactly as I planned. Oh yes, they'll see. Once I have the Doctor's head ...'

She heard him close the draperies and move away from the bed. 'It's getting dark,' he muttered. Sarah guessed he must be staring out of the window. The rambling voice went on. Solon was talking to himself. 'Maren should have sent the head by now. Nothing can have gone wrong. The Doctor must have gone into the Temple. He *must*! I don't understand ... where is that head?'

Sarah heard the restless footsteps pace the floor for a moment, then go out of the door. She started struggling with her bonds, then stopped as other, heavier footsteps came into the laboratory. A beaker of water touched her lips. 'Girl, drink,' rumbled Condo. Obediently Sarah drank.

For a long time Solon wandered restlessly about the castle. Time and again he went to the front door, peering across the darkening plain for one of the Sisterhood bearing the Doctor's head. But no one came. At last, drawn by some irresistible fascination,

Solon re-entered the basement crypt where the brain of Morbius floated in its tank. Immediately Morbius began to interrogate him. 'What is happening, Solon? Is it time for the operation?'

Absently Solon replied, 'Not yet, Morbius. I am still waiting for the Time Lord's head.'

'Time Lord? This Doctor is a *Time Lord*?'

Solon bit his lip. He had deliberately refrained from telling Morbius that the Doctor was a Time Lord, for fear that the news would prove too disturbing for him. But the secret was out now so he might as well put a good face on it. 'Why yes, Morbius. Of course the Doctor is a Time Lord. That's why the head is so perfect for you. From one of your own race, from those who turned on you and tried to destroy you, we obtain a new head, eh Morbius? What you might call the *crowning irony*.' Solon giggled nervously at his own gruesome joke.

'Fool,' said Morbius dispassionately. 'You are a *fool*, Solon. Don't you see what this means? The Time Lords must have got wind of the way we cheated them. They've managed to track me down.'

Solon gasped in sudden panic. 'No ... no you're wrong.'

'I am not wrong,' boomed the commanding voice. 'I know the Time Lords, pallid, devious worms! You had the Doctor here, Solon—and you let him go!'

'The Sisterhood snatched him from me,' babbled Solon. 'Just as I had him helpless, they took him. You think he and Maren have been plotting together? That they pretended to be enemies so as to deceive me?'

'Of course,' said Morbius positively. 'Soon, the Time Lords will return in force to finish their work—and they'll find me here, helpless, defenceless. They'll destroy me, Solon. Thanks to you they'll destroy me with ease ... and all my sufferings will have been for nothing.'

'And what of my work? All my years of terrible loneliness, the isolation.' Solon realised they were both wallowing in useless self-pity. 'What can we *do*, Morbius? How can we stop them?'

'We have only one chance. You must get me away from here before they arrive!'

'But how can I?' Solon gestured towards the tank and its surrounding circuitry. 'The support system is scarcely portable—not for more than very short distances. And without it your brain will die, Morbius.'

'The body you have already made must serve as my support system. You must transplant me into it, Solon, while there is still time.'

Solon shook his head despairingly. 'It isn't possible. Without a suitable head ...'

'You have the girl's head. Use that.'

(On the stairway, Condo heard this and stiffened warily. He paused to listen.)

'The head is too small, Morbius. It's the same problem with Condo. If I put the brain into a braincase too small to contain it you would die, just as surely as at the hands of the Time Lords.'

'Yet I *must* be free of this tank. I must have a head, a body, a physical being again ... Solon, you spoke once of constructing an artificial brain case.'

'I abandoned that project long ago.'

'Why?'

'There were problems ... formidable problems. There was a build-up of static electricity within the cranial cavity. At times of stress it could have earthed through the brain, upsetting the delicate equilibrium, disturbing the neural centres ...'

Impatiently Morbius interrupted, 'But you did make a brain case?'

'Indeed, yes. I still have it here somewhere.' Solon went to a corner locker and rummaged amongst shelves piled high with disintegrating equipment. At last he came up with a large transparent globe, its interior a maze of delicate circuits. From the front projected two photo-cells each on a transparent stalk, the 'eyes' of this artificial head. Solon blew the dust off the contraption and examined it gloomily. 'Oh, it wouldn't do, Morbius. There could be severe pain, seizures, perhaps even madness ...'

There was no hesitation in Morbius's voice. 'Whatever the risks I will take them, rather than surrender to the Time Lords. There is no choice left to me, Solon.'

Solon hesitated, wringing his hands in anguish. But Morbius was right—and Solon knew it. 'Very well, my lord. I shall do my utmost. I shall use all my skill. With luck the brain case will function, at least for a while. Long enough for us to escape and start afresh elsewhere. We shall triumph yet!'

'Prepare me for the operation!'

Obediently Solon moved to the tank controls. He flicked switches, the greenish glow died, and the convoluted purple mass that was the brain of Morbius sank slowly to the bottom of the tank.

The Doctor's body lay in a long, coffin-shaped casket. Ohica touched his forehead. It was icy cold. Two Sisters came forward and closed the casket. The still, calm face of the Doctor could be seen through a transparent panel in the lid.

Maren raised her hand, and four Sisters came forward. They lifted the casket, one at each corner, and stood waiting. Ohica glanced worriedly at the High Priestess. 'Is what we are doing right, High One?'

Maren's voice was implacable. 'Things will fall out as they are ordained. The matter is out of our hands now.' She raised her voice. 'Take the casket to Solon. If he asks questions, tell him we have slain the Doctor, and the body is his to do with as he will.'

Slowly the Sisters carried the casket away.

In Solon's laboratory, Sarah was wrestling grimly with the straps that held her to the chair. Food and drink had renewed her energy, and her determination to escape, or at least to do *something* to hamper Solon's evil schemes. She heard an approaching footstep, abandoned her efforts, and let herself slump back into her chair. 'Solon?' she called. Strange how quickly she was learning to recognise different footsteps.

Solon ignored her. He put the globe-shaped brain case he was carrying onto a bench, went to the four poster bed, and drew back the curtains. He leaned over his monstrous creation and began checking it over. A few minutes later he straightened up, re-drew the curtains, and headed for the door. 'Condo!' he yelled.

Condo appeared in the doorway with suspicious suddenness. He had been trailing Solon around the castle, trying to gain some clue to his Master's in-tentions. Two thoughts were occupying Condo's limited intelligence—Sarah's safety, and the return of his precious arm. Only this latter problem pre-vented him from killing Solon out of hand.

Solon took the prompt appearance of Condo for granted. 'I need your help, Condo. We must prepare for an important operation.'

'Operation to put back arm?'

'Not yet, Condo, though that will be next, I pro-mise you. No, this operation is far more delicate. It concerns the brain of our Master, Morbius.'

Sarah looked up in alarm. *Had* the Doctor's head been delivered to Solon after all? But before she could ask questions, Solon had bustled Condo from the laboratory.

Solon led Condo down the stairs and into the crypt. He went to one side of the now-disconnected tank, and motioned Condo to the other. 'We must hope the liquid will cushion the brain against the shock of moving. Now, get your hook under that edge and lift!'

Struggling and sweating they wrestled the heavy case out of the crypt and up the stairs towards the laboratory. Condo did most of the work, Solon alternately cursing his clumsiness and beseeching him to be more careful. At last they reached the laboratory, and heaved the case up on to a bench.

Condo looked on interestedly as Solon fussed round the tank, checking that the brain had come to no harm. 'Master put brain in body? Where head?'

Solon tapped the transparent globe. 'This will serve as the head, Condo. An artificial head, just like your artificial arm ...'

'Condo see new body. Solon never let Condo see—Condo see now!' Before Solon could stop him, Condo strode across the room and pulled back the curtains around the four-poster bed.

'Condo, come away,' shouted Solon—but he was too late.

Condo was staring in fascinated horror at the creature on the bed. More particularly, he was staring at the brawny and unmistakeably human left arm that joined the shaggy shoulder. He stared at it unbelievingly, then looked down at his own good arm, then at the missing one.

'Condo's arm,' he growled. 'You take Condo's arm—for this?'

Solon tried to bluff. 'I *needed* it, Condo. You remember, we were only able to save one usable claw from that Crustacoid in the wreck ... Look upon it as a loan. You'll have it back as soon as I can find a better. Now hurry, man. The brain will deteriorate if it's not connected soon ...'

Condo wasn't listening. He advanced remorselessly on Solon, hand and hook reaching out. 'You take Condo's arm. Now you die!'

As the hook flashed down, Solon snatched a blaster

from beneath his robes and fired. Condo yelled and staggered back. He stumbled into the life-support tank and sent it crashing to the floor. It shattered and the brain of Morbius floated out like a jelly-fish on a flood of nutrient fluid. 'Murdering peasant!' Solon screamed, and fired again.

Howling with pain and rage, Condo staggered out of the door and away down the corridor. Solon ignored him. Snatching the transparent brain case from the bench he knelt amidst the shattered remnants of the tank and carefully scooped the spongy mass of the brain from the floor and deposited it inside.

Strapped in her chair all this while, Sarah had been listening helplessly to the sound of struggle. 'Solon, what's happening?' she called.

Solon crouched over the brain-case, turning it slowly in his hands, examining the brain within for signs of damage. 'The greatest intellect that has ever been—destroyed by a mindless brute.' Solon began to sob.

Another of Karn's frequent storms was building up. Thunder rumbled, winds howled eerily and occasional flashes of lightning lit up the mountainous landscape. One of these flashes revealed a strange procession wending its way along the valley that led to Solon's castle. Four black-robed Sisters bore a coffin-shaped casket on their shoulders. Before and behind, other Sisters escorted them with blazing torches. Their flames lit up the Doctor's calm and peaceful face.

The ghostly procession moved silently on its way.

Sarah went on shouting at Solon, until at last he regained enough control to answer her. 'There was a dreadful accident. The brain of Morbius was *there* —on the floor! I can't tell what damage there might be ...' A note of decision came into Solon's voice. 'I *must* continue with the operation. You will have to be my assistant, I can't be expected to work alone.'

'What operation?' asked Sarah frantically. 'On the Doctor?'

'No, no, no. The Doctor seems to have disappeared. I'm going to take the brain of Morbius in this artificial case, and fix it to the torso of the body I've created for him. You will help me.'

'Oh no, I won't!'

Sarah felt the cold metal of the blaster against her forehead. 'You'll do as I say,' snapped Solon. He unbuckled her straps. 'Now, get up and come over here.'

'How *can* I help you,' protested Sarah. 'You know I can't see.'

'All you need do is work the air-pump. One stroke every three seconds, do you understand?' Solon thrust what felt like the handle of a small stirrup-pump into Sarah's hand.

'All right, I'll try. Suppose I make a mistake?'

Carefully Solon began adjusting the position of the brain inside the transparent case. 'It's very simple, my dear. If Morbius dies, then you die. Now, shall we begin? You are privileged to assist at a great moment in medical history.'

Solon worked like a maniac in the tense time that followed. First he connected the brain to the neural harness in the transparent case. Then the case itself was joined to the monstrous torso. He worked swiftly, pausing only to wipe the sweat from his eyes, connecting the plastic 'head' to the assembled body with a laser-scalpel. It was a fantastically delicate operation, carried out under primitive conditions, and with amazing speed.

Sarah of course saw nothing of this. But she could feel the tension in the air and hear the hoarse breathing of the Monster. Solon rapped out an instruction. 'The pressure! I told you every three seconds, girl.' Hurriedly Sarah worked the pump.

At last she sensed that Solon had stopped working. 'There! The casing's connected to the neural harness, and the links are complete. All I need do now is to test for neural feedback.'

'Can I stop pumping now?'

'Yes, of course.'

Thankfully Sarah straightened up. She heard Solon moving, and then he gave an excited gasp. 'There, did you see that? The claw twitched.'

'I can't see anything, Solon. But that mixed-up monster of yours had the twitches when I first met it.'

Solon sniffed indignantly. '*Those* were just random nervous reflexes. But this was a positive response to stimulation. Just what I'd hoped for!'

'The operation's succeeded then?'

Solon rubbed his hands triumphantly. 'The motor centres of the brain have taken control. If there was no cerebral damage, then in a matter of minutes Morbius will live again!'

There came a rusty, jangling noise from below. It was the bell that hung by the front door. Sarah remembered the Doctor sounding it when they'd first arrived.

Solon tensed. 'What was that?'

'Front door bell,' said Sarah practically. 'Milkman, perhaps? No, it's too late for that. Maybe it's the evening paper!'

Solon rounded on her. 'Stop babbling and go and answer it, girl!'

'Look, I'm not signing on as your permanent assistant,' said Sarah spiritedly. 'Anyway, I can't see!'

She heard Solon sigh. 'All right. Stay here. Don't move—and don't touch anything or it'll be the worse for you!' She heard him hurry out.

Everything went quiet. Sarah heard only the distant rumbling of the thunder, and the hoarse breathing of the thing on the bed. She couldn't see that the round globe of its head had suddenly swung round, so that the projecting photo-cells pointed straight at her. Nor did she hear the movement as the creature on the bed sat upright, then got slowly to its feet.

Sarah had suddenly found that she could see a tiny glowing point of light hanging before her eyes. Totally absorbed she sat staring into space. The ghastly monstrosity that was Solon's creation, crowned now with a transparent globe for a head, lurched slowly towards her, flexing its one giant claw ...

10

Monster on the Rampage

Solon ran down the stairs and into the great hall. The main door stood open and an icy wind howled through the room. There was no one in the hall ... but a long, coffin-shaped casket lay in the centre of the floor. Suddenly the doors slammed shut, as if of their own accord.

Solon crossed to the casket and peered through the transparent panel in the lid. The Doctor's face looked impassively back at him. Solon heaved the lid from the casket and placed a hand on the Doctor's forehead, lifted a wrist feeling for a pulse. 'Dead,' he muttered. 'The Sisters accepted my bargain after all.' Suddenly he realised. 'Morbius was wrong ... If we'd waited. If we'd only waited ...' After the tension of the recent operation, the irony of the situation was too much for Solon. Clutching the side of the casket for support, he collapsed into hysterical laughter.

Sarah sat quite still, staring straight ahead of her. She was still gazing in fascination at the tiny point of light. It grew brighter, clearer ... and resolved itself into an old-fashioned Bunsen burner left alight on Solon's laboratory bench. She could *see*—the flame, the burner, the bench, and a misty outline of the room beyond. The blindness was going as swiftly as it had come. She could see again!

Sarah was so absorbed, and so overjoyed, that she didn't hear the sounds of stealthy movement behind her. She rubbed her fists in her eyes then looked again. She could see. She could really see!

Then she heard a dragging footstep. She turned to see the Monster looming threateningly over her.

Sarah backed away. The Morbius Monster made a clumsy grab at her, missed and knocked over the Bunsen burner. It fell into a tray of surgical spirits in which some of Solon's instruments lay sterilising. Immediately a sheet of flame shot up. The Monster swiped wildly at the tray, sending blazing liquid flying through the air. Some of it splashed on its own hide and set it alight. The Monster staggered back, roaring in rage and pain.

Sarah dodged round it, and ran towards the stairs. Behind her the Monster began smashing up the laboratory of its creator with a methodical fury.

Solon heard the noise from above and ran to the staircase, bumping into Sarah who was on her way down. He grabbed her shoulders. 'What is it? What's *happening* up there?'

Sarah pulled herself free. 'You'd better do something, Solon. Your friend's on the rampage!'

Solon stared wildly at her. 'No, not yet. It's much too soon, there must be a period of complete rest. I'll go and stop him.'

Too taken aback to register that Sarah was no longer blind, Solon ran up the staircase. Sarah watched him go, shaking her head. From what she'd seen it was going to take more than Solon's best bedside manner to calm the Monster down. Still, that was Solon's worry and he was welcome to it.

Sarah turned towards the door—and stopped at the sight of the sinister-looking casket. She ran across to it and looked inside. 'Doctor!'

The Doctor opened one eye. 'Hullo, Sarah,' he said calmly.

He climbed out of the casket like a very cheerful ghost, and Sarah flung herself into his arms. 'I thought ... I thought ...' she sobbed.

'You thought I was dead?' finished the Doctor. 'You know, you're always making that mistake!'

Sarah wiped her eyes. 'Well if you're not dead, what are you doing in a coffin?' she demanded logically.

The Doctor chuckled. 'It was all the help I could persuade the Sisters to give me. I put myself into suspended animation and they delivered me in a coffin to put Solon off his guard. Now come on, Sarah, we've got to find the brain of Morbius. Solon wants to bring him back to life again, and he's got to be stopped. We'll search the castle.' The Doctor prepared to dash off, but Sarah didn't move.

'You're too late, Doctor.' There came a screaming and smashing from upstairs. She glanced towards the sound. 'I'm afraid Morbius is already up and about!'

The Doctor looked at her severely. 'Too late, am I? My dear Sarah, I think you'd better tell me what's been going on.'

*

Solon's laboratory was now a total wreck. Every piece of equipment was smashed and even the heavy lab benches were overturned.

The Monster lurched through the broken wreckage to find itself facing a long mirror. For the moment the creature stared in horror at its own reflection. Then with a roar of anger, it wrenched the mirror from the wall and smashed it to the floor, shattering it to pieces. Solon ran in, and looked in horror at the devastation all around him. 'My work ... my experiments ... What are you *doing*, Morbius?'

The Monster swung round and Solon backed away. 'Morbius, this is Solon, your creator. Can you hear me?'

The only answer was a guttural roar.

'Morbius, it is just as I feared,' cried Solon. 'The speech centre isn't functioning. The brain may be damaged. You *must* let me examine you ...'

The Monster roared again and moved closer. Its movements were smoother now, and better co-ordinated. Suddenly it pounced, gripping Solon in a crushing bear-hug. Solon screamed. 'No, Morbius, don't! I *made* you ... don't you recognise me? Morbius, *no* ...'

Solon's voice trailed away as a final vicious squeeze drove the breath from his body, and he slumped back unconscious. The Monster shook the limp body for a moment, and then threw it to one side. Morbius swung round and moved out of the laboratory.

Sarah came to the end of a hasty and garbled recital

of all that had been happening to her, finishing with an account of the Morbius Monster now rampaging about above their heads.

The Doctor shook his head incredulously. 'A glass brain-case you say? Dear me!'

Sarah waved an impatient hand. 'Glass, plastic, I don't know. The thing looks like an upside-down goldfish bowl. You can actually *see* Morbius's brain inside it.'

'Good grief.' The Doctor shook his head wonderingly. 'I say, maybe we'll be able to read his thoughts.'

'This is serious, Doctor. The whole thing's horribly serious.'

The Doctor nodded. 'Crude and inefficient as well. The brain might malfunction ... and that could be dangerous.'

The Doctor saw that Sarah was staring over his shoulder in horror. He swung round. The Monster was creeping soundlessly down the staircase towards them.

The Doctor took Sarah's arm. 'Now keep calm, Sarah. Keep calm.' He glanced down at her. She was quite still, rigid with fear. 'That's right,' said the Doctor approvingly, 'you *are* calm. '

The Doctor managed a welcoming smile as the Monster loomed over them. 'Hullo, Morbius. You remember me ...'

Whether the Monster remembered the Doctor or not, it didn't seem to be interested in a reunion. It floored the Doctor with a sudden slash of the clawed arm, then turned its attention to Sarah.

Sarah turned to run. But the Monster was too quick

for her. It sidled round in front of her and began stalking her round the hall, always blocking any attempt at escape. Sarah screamed ...

On a nearby landing, the half-conscious Condo heard her cries and staggered to his feet. He had been badly wounded by Solon's blaster, and, animal-like, had crawled into a dark corner to recover or to die. Such was his strength and vitality, that he was able to climb to his feet and stagger down the staircase towards the hall.

Sarah was running for the stairs, the Monster close behind, when Condo appeared, thrust her out of the way and grappled with the Monster. Such was Condo's strength that, wounded as he was, he was able for a time to hold his own against the Monster. The two giants reeled about the hall, both roaring with rage. Their combined bulk crashed into Sarah and sent her rolling down the stairs to the crypt, to land half-stunned at the bottom.

Shaking his head, the Doctor started clambering to his feet.

Condo and the Monster, locked in a death grip, staggered across the hall, splintered a heavy wooden table, and crashed to the ground, where they rolled over and over, still fighting savagely. Condo managed to draw his sword and hacked savagely at the Monster. With a scream of rage, the Monster smashed the blade aside and the huge claw clamped onto Condo's throat, slowly throttling the life out of him.

By the time the Doctor had staggered to his feet,

the Monster had risen to its feet, casting Condo's lifeless body aside. It gave a bellow of triumph, then lurched towards the front door, flinging it open and disappearing into the night. The Doctor watched it go with heartfelt relief, and started looking round for Sarah. Eventually he found her lying half-dazed at the bottom of the stairs. He picked her up and carried her into the crypt, laying her down on an empty laboratory bench.

After a moment, Sarah opened her eyes, tried to sit up, and saw the Doctor frowning down at her. 'Are you all right?'

'More or less.' Sarah sat up and looked round. 'What happened? Where's that ... thing?'

'Gone for a lurch, I think,' said the Doctor cheerfully.

'What about Condo?'

'I'm afraid it killed him.'

Sarah shuddered. It hadn't exactly been a beautiful friendship, but Condo had saved her life on at least two occasions, and it saddened her to hear of his death.

Abruptly the Doctor said, 'I'd better take a look around, see what happened to Solon. Stay here, I won't be long.'

Before Sarah could argue he was gone. She thought of following him but a sudden tiredness overcame her. She decided to lie back and close her eyes, just for a moment. Soon she was fast asleep.

Solon picked himself up slowly and painfully, hugging

his sore ribs, rubbing the bruise on his forehead. He staggered through the wreckage of his laboratory to a wall locker, took out some hollow metal darts and filled them with a colourless fluid from a syringe. Wincing at the pain from his ribs, he made his way slowly downstairs and into the ruined hall. He looked at the wreckage, turned over Condo's body with his foot, then went to a wall cupboard. He unlocked it and took out a strangely shaped rifle, loading it with the plastic darts. As he turned, his eye was caught by the casket, and with a sudden shock he realised that it was empty. He was still staring at it when a mocking voice behind him said, 'It's one of those nights, isn't it, Solon?'

Solon turned to see a tall figure leaning against the doorway that led to the stairs. 'Doctor,' he stammered. 'I thought ... '

'You thought I was nicely dead, didn't you? A gift-wrapped present from the Sisters.'

The mention of the Sisterhood reminded Solon of his main preoccupation. 'Morbius has gone, Doctor. He must be stopped.'

'He should never have been started,' said the Doctor severely.

Obsessed with the fate of his beloved creation, Solon didn't seem to hear him. 'His brain is functioning only on the most primitive level,' he explained earnestly. 'You must help me find him, Doctor.'

'Must I really?' The Doctor looked thoughtfully at Solon, realising that this strange man was so single-minded he was trying to enlist him as an ally.

Solon seemed to assume that everyone shared his

concern for his monstrous creation. 'It's the Sister-hood, you see, Doctor. Hatred for the Sisters is Morbius's most basic emotion at the moment.' Solon's voice dropped into a lecturer's tone. 'You see, at the instinctual level on which his mind is now functioning, that hatred is virtually certain to manifest itself as animal aggression.'

'Oh wrap up, Solon,' said the Doctor inelegantly. Solon lapsed into an offended silence. The Doctor looked at him in a sort of amused disgust. The funny thing was that Solon was quite right. They *were* allies of a kind, at least until Morbius was found. 'All right, Solon, come on,' said the Doctor finally. He led the way out into the night.

Activated by the hatred in the half-crazed brain of Morbius, the Monster staggered through the stormy night, heading by an unerring instinct for the Temple of the Sisterhood. From time to time it paused to roar defiance at the lightning overhead, then lurched determinedly on its way.

The Doctor and Solon followed close behind. Since they already knew its destination they had no need to bother to track it. They simply headed for the Temple themselves by the most direct route, hoping to cut the Monster's trail somewhere on the way.

They came at last to the boulder strewn slopes that overlooked the entrance to the cave. The Doctor paused and looked round. 'No sign of it. Either it's here already or we've arrived first. We'd better split up.'

Solon nodded silently and disappeared amongst the rocks. The Doctor moved off in the other direction.

It was the custom of the Sisters to spend an occasional night in meditation, keeping a kind of vigil. It was for this reason that a Sister called Kelia was standing motionless among the rocks, gazing raptly at the storm clouds that filled the sky.

Her keen senses heard the rattle of a displaced stone. She turned unhurriedly, expecting to see one of the Sisterhood come to share her vigil. The sight of the dome-headed horror that confronted her shook her from her semi-trance, but she had time for no more than a single scream before the great claw closed on her throat ...

The Doctor and Solon both heard the choked cry and ran towards the sound. By the time they arrived, there was only a black-robed figure crumpled at the base of the boulder. The Doctor knelt to examine it, then looked up, shaking his head. 'Dead. The neck's broken. It can't be far away, Solon. Let's split up again, maybe we can corner him in these rocks.'

But it wasn't the Monster who was cornered. The Doctor made his way cautiously between the boulders, peering into the darkness. He paused to listen, but there was only the rumble of thunder, the eerie moaning of the night-wind. He didn't see the monstrous shape that loomed up behind him ... As the claw reached out Solon appeared on top of a nearby rock. 'Look out, Doctor!' he screamed. The Doctor turned and the Monster lunged forward. Solon threw the rifle to his shoulder and fired at the Monster's back.

There was a 'phutt!' of compressed air, then another. The Monster twitched, half-turned, then returned to the attack. It lurched onto the Doctor who collapsed beneath its weight. He struggled furiously, then realised that the Monster hadn't so much *jumped* on him as *fallen* on him. It was lying motionless, breathing in deep snoring gasps.

The Doctor wriggled out from beneath the Monster's bulk, to find Solon anxiously leaning over them with a torch. 'At least there's no damage, as far as I can tell.'

'Damage?' asked the Doctor, picking himself up. 'No. I think I'm all right!' Then he realised that Solon was concerned only for the Monster.

'There may be some slight contusions,' Solon was murmuring. 'I'll know better when I get him home.'

The Doctor grabbed Solon's arm and pulled him to his feet. 'Do you realise, Solon, that this abomination you've created has just broken somebody's neck?'

Solon waved away this unimportant detail. 'Simple animal instinct, Doctor. If Morbius was rational, he'd be very careful not to antagonise the Sisterhood— not at this stage. Help me up with him, would you?'

The Doctor helped Solon to get the slumbering Monster to its feet. 'Come along, Doctor,' said Solon sharply. 'We *must* get him back to the laboratory before the anaesthetic-dart wears off.'

The Doctor took a firmer grip on the Monster. 'All right, Solon. But when we do get him back, he's not going out again. He isn't going anywhere—ever!'

Solon heaved the Monster round. 'What do you mean, Doctor?'

'I mean this little experiment of yours is going to end where it began—on your operating table. As for the brain, it can be disconnected and returned to the Time Lords.'

Solon made no reply as they staggered off, the inert bulk of the Monster supported between them. But there was a look on his face which suggested that his brief alliance with the Doctor would soon be over.

When Ohica learned of the death of Kelia she ordered the body to be brought before Maren in the Temple. The old High Priestess glared down angrily at the crumpled form. 'Who is responsible, Ohica? Who killed Kelia, our Sister?'

'She was found just outside the caves, High One. The guards report seeing a monstrous creature moving amongst the rocks. Others saw Solon and the Doctor hunting for it.'

'So—Solon has succeeded in his vile experiments!'

'So it would seem, High One. And if the Doctor is right, Solon will have given this Monster the brain of our ancient enemy, Morbius.'

'If this is so—then our Sisterhood faces its greatest crisis. What should we do, Ohica?'

Ohica stared at her in astonishment. It was the first time she had ever seen the High One express any kind of doubt.

The Monster lay stretched out on the laboratory

bench, with Solon hovering solicitously over it. The Doctor paused in the doorway. 'I'll give you five minutes, Solon. Five minutes and no more.'

Solon looked up, an expression of anguish on his face. 'Doctor, you're asking me to destroy the work of a lifetime.'

There was no sympathy in the Doctor's voice. 'You've spent a lifetime attempting to resurrect evil. Now, if you won't disconnect that brain, I'll do it myself.' The Doctor grabbed a hacksaw from a litter of instruments on the floor, and advanced towards the Monster. 'Though I warn you, my surgical techniques are a bit rough and ready.'

Solon shuddered, waving him away. 'I'll do it, Doctor, I promise.'

The Doctor threw down the saw. 'Five minutes, Solon—and I'll be back to count the pieces!'

The Doctor marched off, the gun tucked under his arm. Solon paused for a minute, then crept down the corridor after him. His face was a mask of hatred.

11

Deathlock!

When the Doctor entered the crypt Sarah was sound asleep on the bench. He gave her a gentle shake. Sarah opened her eyes and stared sleepily at him. She yawned, and propped herself up on one elbow. 'D'you know, Doctor, I've been having the most terrible dream. More like a kind of nightmare really. First I was blinded, then I was attacked by something that looked as if it was made of butcher's left-overs.'

The Doctor grinned. 'No doubt you were knocked down a flight of stairs as well?'

'How did you know?'

'I was there!'

Sarah sat up and looked around her. 'So it was all real, then? What happened to Mister Allsorts?'

'We managed to track him down. Solon's dismantling him now.'

Sarah raised her eyebrows. 'Just like that? I'm surprised he didn't raise more of a fuss.'

The Doctor smiled grimly, tapping the gun. 'I'm afraid I insisted. We're lucky he botched the initial operation. The brain of Morbius in a body like that makes a terrifying combination. I've got to see Solon destroy his handiwork, for the sake of the entire universe.'

'Morbius was really that dangerous?'

'Morbius?' The Doctor's face was grave. 'You've seen this planet, Sarah. Some of it anyway. Well, there was a great civilisation here once. And this is just one of many other such planets. All destroyed because of Morbius, nothing but ashes left behind ...'

The Doctor moved to the door. 'I'd better go and see if he's finished.' He tried to open the door but it was locked. 'It seems I underestimated Solon. I thought he was thoroughly cowed. He's sneaked down after us and locked us in.'

'Tit for tat—I did the same to him! Now how do we get out of here? Sonic screwdriver?'

The Doctor patted his pockets. 'Left it in the TARDIS.'

'Shoot the lock out?'

'With a dart-gun? I'm sorry, Sarah, but for the moment we seem to be well and truly trapped.'

Listening from the other side of the door, Solon smiled in satisfaction and hurried back to his laboratory. Hastily he set about salvaging his instruments, and assembling an operating set-up. Laser scalpel in hand he approached the sleeping Monster. 'This time, Morbius, I promise you, there will be no mistakes!'

Maren sat impassively on her throne. Beside her Ohica spoke, in a low pleading voice. 'Is it just, High One, that we should let the Doctor fight our battles for us? Morbius is our enemy also.'

'There is no proof, Ohica, that the brain of Morbius survives. That was simply the Doctor's theory.'

'A theory which gives meaning to the experiments

of Solon. And now we have the death of Kelia to avenge! Morbius is sworn to destroy us—there will be other deaths unless he is stopped.'

Still Maren hesitated. 'Away from the Flame, without the Circle of Power, our powers fade. There is little we can do.'

'Then let us do the little that we can,' said Ohica fiercely. 'Otherwise the Doctor faces Morbius *and* Solon alone—while we do nothing.'

Maren's voice quavered. 'I am old, Ohica, old, and my courage fails me. I am too weak to leave the Temple. *I* cannot lead you.'

Ohica's eyes blazed. 'Then let me, High One. Give the order, and let me lead the Sisterhood against Morbius!'

Sarah was pacing about the crypt, looking for hidden passageways or convenient chimneys. There was nothing. She turned impatiently to the Doctor who sat glumly, chin in hands. 'Come on, Doctor, there must be something you can do. It's not like you to give up. Solon's got to be stopped somehow.'

The Doctor pointed upwards. 'There are thousands of tons of stone between Solon's laboratory and where we are ...' He stopped abruptly. 'Wait a minute, I've got an idea ...'

Sarah brightened. 'I knew you would.'

The Doctor was rummaging amongst the racks of chemicals that lined the walls. 'Solon must have kept the brain alive in a colloidal nutrient ... Ah!' The Doctor grabbed a flask and held it up triumphantly.

'Hydrogen cyanide ...' He found another flask. 'And prussic acid!' The Doctor examined several flasks, nodding thoughtfully as he checked the contents.

'So what are we going to do? Mix a cocktail and drink ourselves to death?'

The Doctor pulled a rack of shelves away from the wall to reveal a tiny ventilation-duct. He wrenched off its cover and held his hand to the vent. 'Splendid, a powerful up-draught ...'

Sarah peered into the tiny space. 'How did you know that would be there?'

'Before Solon took this place over for his castle, it probably housed a hydrogen reactor. I know how they're designed.'

'Well, what are we going to do?'

Suddenly the Doctor's face was very grave. 'I'm pretty sure this duct will lead to Solon's laboratory, Sarah. And we have everything here we need to make a pretty nasty mixture of gases.'

Sarah said slowly, 'Are you suggesting ...'

The Doctor nodded. 'I'm afraid so, Sarah. I can't say I like the idea ... but unless Solon is stopped— it will mean the deaths of untold millions. So stand clear—and I mean *well* clear. There's probably more danger to us than there is to Solon.'

In his laboratory Solon was hard at work, changing and re-adjusting the connections that linked the brain of Morbius to its artificial container, and to the Monster's body. With the malfunctions corrected, there was no reason why the brain shouldn't function

9

properly. Absorbed in his delicate task, Solon failed to notice a thin thread of greyish vapour that drifted from the air duct . . .

A water-soaked handkerchief over his mouth, the Doctor was using his hat to fan a metal beaker of bubbling liquid. From it rose a thick grey vapour, which was promptly sucked into the ventilation duct.

On the far side of the room, Sarah, a similar handkerchief over her own mouth, looked on. In a muffled voice she called, 'How will we know if it's worked?'

'Well if Solon succeeds he's bound to bring Morbius down for a gloat. So if we don't get any visitors by a month's time . . .'

'We'll know it's worked?'

'Right!' The Doctor shoved the smoking beaker into the air-duct, grabbed a pile of water-soaked rags and blocked the opening to stop the gas drifting back. 'Well, either it's worked or it hasn't. All we can do now is wait and see.'

Solon finished his last connection and straightened up. He moved to an electrical booster apparatus connected to the Monster's chest, and threw the switch. There was a surge of power. The Monster stirred, and slowly began to sit up.

'Solon?' it said. 'Solon?' The voice was that of Morbius.

Exultantly Solon said, 'I am here! I've succeeded, Morbius. You live! You live again!'

A fit of coughing racked Solon as the vapour from the ventilator reached him. 'Morbius,' he gasped. 'Morbius ...' He pitched forward onto his face.

The Monster on the bench, now truly Morbius at last, sat up and swung its legs from the bench. It studied the body of Solon, the gas drifting from the ventilator.

'Gas,' said Morbius. 'How ingenious, Doctor.' There was amusement in the deep, compelling voice. Morbius stretched, looked around. Then, completely at home in his new body, he strode confidently from the laboratory.

Sarah was still prowling restlessly about the crypt. She paused before a complicated electronic set-up. A framework of shining girders supported a circular central screen. Two head-sets were linked to it, one on each side. 'What's all this, Doctor?'

The Doctor crossed to stand beside her. 'Well, well, well, a mind-bending set-up. One of Morbius's favourite toys. Solon must have kept it as a souvenir from the good old days.' He examined the apparatus more closely. 'All linked up and ready to go, I see.'

'What does it do?'

'It enables two opponents to match the force of their minds in direct confrontation. Morbius used to boast that he'd never been beaten.'

'Is it dangerous?'

'Not if it's played for fun. But played to the ultimate —it can end in a mental deathlock. The winner can *think* his opponent to death by driving him back to the moment of birth—then beyond. Care for a little game?'

Sarah shuddered. 'No thanks, I don't think I'll risk it.' She began pacing the room again. 'How many seconds in a month, Doctor?'

'Two million, six hundred and seventy-eight thousand, four hundred,' said the Doctor—and they heard the key turn in the lock.

'Short month,' said Sarah nervously. The door opened and the Morbius monster stood in the doorway. The Doctor grabbed for the dart-gun, but with incredible speed Morbius snatched it from him and smashed it against the wall. The Doctor backed away, impressed by the speed of his opponent's reflexes. This time there was no doubt that the operation had been successful.

'Your idea was ingenious, Doctor, but ineffectual. Your gas affected only Solon. In my new form, I have the lungs of a Birastrop.'

'With a built-in filter system.' The Doctor nodded thoughtfully. With deliberate rudeness he added, 'How does it feel to be the biggest mongrel in the universe?'

Morbius laughed scornfully. 'Solon assembled this body for efficiency, not appearance. To be free again —that is all that matters.'

'Free to cause more havoc, more destruction?'

'The Time Lords will not prevail against me this time—nor the Sisterhood. When it is learned that Morbius has cheated death, my followers will rise in their milliards!'

There was total certainty in the deep voice. The

worst of it was, reflected the Doctor ruefully, Morbius was very probably right. Somehow he had to shake that arrogant self-confidence. Mockingly he said, 'Still, you'll have to stop calling yourself Morbius, won't you? I mean, there's precious little Morbius left now. Let's think of a new name for you. Pot-pourri would be appropriate.'

Realising that for some reason the Doctor was trying to make Morbius lose his temper, Sarah joined in. 'What about chop-suey?'

Quickly the Doctor said, 'That's very good, Sarah. Chop-suey the galactic emperor.'

Morbius took a quick pace towards him, and the Doctor jumped back.

'Enjoy your joke, Doctor. *You* will be the first to die!'

'Now, now,' said the Doctor reprovingly. 'Mustn't get the old brain overheated, must we? You want to take care—it's not as strong as it was!'

'My brain functions perfectly!'

'I doubt it, Morbius. All that time in the tank, it's bound to have gone a little soft. I say, would you care to put it to the test? How about a small game of mind-bending? We have all the apparatus here.'

At last Sarah saw the Doctor's plan. 'No, Doctor, you mustn't,' she called. The Doctor ignored her.

'I challenge you, Morbius! Well, what do you say?'

The photo-electric cell that served Morbius for eyes surveyed the apparatus. 'I am a Time Lord of the first rank, Doctor. What are you?'

'Oh *I'm* nothing,' said the Doctor hastily. 'A mere

133

nobody. But you see, Morbius, I don't think you're in the first rank any more.'

Morbius stepped forward and fixed the headset to his transparent brain-case. 'Very well, Doctor if that is how you choose to die. I accept your challenge.'

'Now there's a sporting gentleman,' said the Doctor cheerfully. But inside he was far from lighthearted. He knew he stood little chance of defeating Morbius. His only hope was that the tremendous stresses of the game would expose some of the hidden weaknesses left by Solon's operation.

The Doctor put on his headset. 'To the death, Morbius?'

'To the death, Doctor. I, Morbius, do not play games.'

'Nor I,' said the Doctor grimly. 'Are you ready? On guard!'

The Doctor and Morbius braced themselves, gripping the gleaming scaffolding. Sarah saw a swirl of images on the central screen. A familiar face appeared—the face they had seen depicted on Solon's clay head. Morbius gave a cry of rage—clearly the appearance of 'his' face was a sign that he was losing.

Morbius rallied, and the face of the Doctor appeared on the screen.

Sarah saw that the real Doctor's face was twisted with effort. Drops of perspiration covered his forehead. Another face appeared on the screen, the debonair white-haired features of the Doctor, as Sarah had first known him.

'You are going, Doctor, going!' roared Morbius

triumphantly. 'How far, Doctor? How long have you lived?'

Yet another Doctor appeared on the screen—a dark-haired little man with a whimsical expression. Then another face ... a proud-looking old man. Exultantly Morbius shouted, 'Your puny mind is powerless against the brain of Morbius. Back, Doctor, back to your beginnings. To your birth—and to your death!' Sarah had a confused impression of even more faces on the screen. The Doctor was groaning, clutching the scaffolding for support ...

Morbius gave a sudden terrible scream. There was a blue flash, and the transparent brain-case filled with smoke. The Doctor pulled himself upright and smiled weakly. Static electricity had fused the circuits in the brain-case, and Morbius was reduced once more to a mindless Monster. The last thing the Doctor saw was the Monster lurching out of the open door. Then blackness swallowed him up.

Sarah ran to the Doctor as he fell from the scaffolding. She tried to lift him to his feet, but he collapsed on the floor.

Sarah felt for his pulse, but she could feel nothing. Sobbing she remembered the Doctor's words, 'The winner can think his opponent to death.' Had Morbius triumphed, even in defeat?

For some time now a procession of black-robed figures had been making its way towards Solon's castle. They carried flaming torches which flared high in the night winds.

They reached the castle at last, and entered the hall just as the Monster stumbled up from the crypt. Seeing them, the Monster roared its hatred and charged through them, disappearing into the night.

Ohica raised her hand in silent command. All but four of the Sisters followed the Monster into the night. Ohica and the others descended the stairs into the crypt, where they found Sarah kneeling by the body of the Doctor. She jumped up at the sight of the sinister figures, but Ohica's voice was kind. 'What has happened?'

'I think he's dying. He took on Morbius in a mental wrestling match.'

Ohica examined the Doctor briefly, then gestured to the Sisters. 'Place the Time Lord within the casket, and bear him back to the Temple.' She turned to Sarah. 'We shall do everything that we can ... but I fear it is too late. He is already dying ...'

The black-robed Sisters with their flaming torches hunted the Monster across the rocky face of Karn. They followed it as it made for the Temple. More torch-carrying Sisters flooded from the caves cutting off its retreat. Blazing torches hemmed the Monster in a circle of fire through which it dared not break.

The encircling flames drove the Monster higher and higher. Their minds linked in telepathic communion, the silent Sisters worked as one, guided by old Maren who sat motionless on her throne, her face blank, seeing through their eyes. 'Higher, sisters, higher,' she ordered—and the Monster was driven to the very peak of the mountain.

Here it turned at bay, snarling and roaring, a semi-circle of blazing torches in front, a sheer precipice behind. The torches came closer and closer. The Monster retreated, back and back ...

Suddenly all the blazing torches seemed to merge into one giant flame. As that flame lunged forward, the Monster screamed and jumped back into empty space. The scream tailed away, down and down, till the misshapen body was smashed to pieces on the jagged rocks far below.

In the Temple, Maren whispered, 'It is done, Sisters. Return!'

The Sisters filed down the mountainside, and the light of their torches was quenched in the sacred cave.

A Time Lord Spell

The Doctor lay silent and unmoving on a kind of bier before Maren's throne. At a respectful distance, some of the Sisters were softly chanting. Sarah looked enquiringly at Ohica. 'They sing the death song,' said the priestess gently. 'It is a sacred chant, sung only when a Time Lord dies.'

Sarah gave her an anguished look. 'Isn't there anything you can do?'

Suddenly Maren spoke. 'Only the Elixir of Life can save him.'

'And we have none,' said Ohica.

Maren seemed to come to a decision. She rose and hobbled slowly across to the bronze gates, unlocked them and flung them open. Fiery and beautiful, the sacred Flame burned strongly in its bowl of rock. Maren lifted the silver chalice from its resting place and looked inside. A few precious drops of the Elixir had formed on its rim. 'A little Elixir has formed, Ohica—a very little. Yet perhaps it may be enough to save the Doctor.'

Ohica hesitated. 'But your own need, High One. Unless you have the Elixir soon ... It will take too long for more to form ...'

'Take it,' commanded the imperious old voice. 'I grow weary of stagnation, Ohica. The Doctor was right. It is time there was an end—a *change* ...'

Ohica took the chalice, leaned over the Doctor, and poured the few precious drops it contained into his mouth. The Doctor licked his lips, then said distinctly, 'Stewed apricots ... what, no custard?' He started to sit up, and Sarah rushed to hug him. The Doctor smiled. 'I know, Sarah, I know you thought I was dead again.' He smacked his lips. 'Great stuff, that Elixir. Fortunately, a little goes a long way!'

They heard Ohica scream, 'Maren, no!'

Sarah turned to see that Maren was actually standing in the basin of the Sacred Flame. The Flame played around her, like a fountain, and she stood smiling in the middle of it. For a moment she changed into a beautiful young woman, smiling and erect. The Flame roared up, concealing her, and when it died down the basin was empty. Ohica bowed her head. 'Maren has sacrificed herself to the Flame.' She picked up the bronze key from the floor, and closed and locked the gates.

Still a little unsteady, the Doctor said, 'Was that the last of the Elixir?'

Sarah nodded. 'You'd have died without it.'

Ohica came towards them, and the Doctor said simply, 'I'm sorry ...'

'It was ordained,' said Ohica quietly. 'Maren died as she had chosen.'

'And Morbius?'

'The Monster too is destroyed. We owe you our thanks, Doctor. Without your help ...'

Hurriedly the Doctor rose to his feet. 'Please, no speeches of gratitude,' he said modestly. 'Sarah and I have to be on our way, don't we, Sarah?'

'Oh yes,' agreed Sarah. Karn was one place she couldn't wait to be away from—and the quicker the better.

The Doctor marched her across to the TARDIS, and unlocked the door. 'Say goodbye to the Sisters, Sarah.'

'Goodbye, Sisters,' said Sarah obediently.

'Goodbye, Sisters,' echoed the Doctor. He unlocked the TARDIS door, then paused to fish something from his pocket and hand it to Ohica.

Ohica stared in amazement at the two brightly coloured cylinders. 'What are these, Doctor?'

'One Thunderclap, one Mighty Atom,' replied the Doctor cheerfully. 'Just in case you have any more trouble with the chimney!' And he ushered Sarah inside the TARDIS.

Ohica was peering closely at the cylinders. 'There is some ancient writing here, Doctor,' she called. 'What does it say? Is it a Time Lord spell?'

The TARDIS doors were already closing, but the Doctor's voice floated clearly from inside. 'Light the blue touch paper and retire immediately ...'

The doors closed, there was a wheezing groaning sound, and the TARDIS faded away.

DOCTOR WHO

Δ	0426118936	PHILIP HINCHCLIFFE Doctor Who and the Masque of Mandragora	85p
	0426201329	TERRANCE DICKS Doctor Who and the Monster of Peladon	85p
Δ	0426201302	Doctor Who and the Nightmare of Eden	85p
˙Δ	0426112520	Doctor Who and the Planet of the Daleks	75p
Δ	0426106555	Dr Who and the Planet of the Spiders	85p
Δ	0426201019	Doctor Who and the Power of Kroll	85p
Δ	0426200616	Doctor Who and the Robots of Death	90p
Δ	042611308X	MALCOLM HULKE Doctor Who and the Sea Devils	90p
Δ	0426116585	PHILIP HINCHCLIFFE Doctor Who and the Seeds of Doom	85p
Δ	0426200497	IAN MARTER Doctor Who and the Sontaren Experiment	60p
Δ	0426110331	MALCOLM HULKE Doctor Who and the Space War	85p
Δ	0426200993	TERRANCE DICKS Doctor Who and the Stones of Blood	75p
Δ	0426119738	TERRANCE DICKS Doctor Who and the Talons of Weng Chiang	75p
Δ	0426110684	GERRY DAVIS Doctor Who and the Tenth Planet	85p

'DOCTOR WHO'

Δ	0426115007	TERRANCE DICKS Doctor Who and the Terror of the Autons	75p
Δ	0426115783	Doctor Who and the Three Doctors	85p
Δ	0426200233	Doctor Who and the Time Warrior	75p
Δ	0426200683	TERRANCE DICKS Doctor Who and the Underworld	75p
Δ	0426200829	MALCOLM HULKE Doctor Who and the War Games	85p
Δ	0426110846	TERRANCE DICKS Doctor Who and the Web of Fear	75p
	0426200675	TERRANCE DICKS The Adventures of K9 and other Mechanical Creatures (illus)	75p
	0426200950	Terry Nation's Dalek Special (illus)	95p
	0426200012	The Second Doctor Who Monster Book (Colour illus)	70p
	0426118421	Doctor Who Dinosaur Book (illus)	75p

DOCTOR WHO

	0426200020	Doctor Who Discovers Prehistoric Animals (NF) (illus)	75p
	0426200039	Doctor Who Discovers Space Travel (NF) (illus)	75p
	0426200047	Doctor Who Discovers Strange and Mysterious Creatures (NF) (illus)	75p
	042620008X	Doctor Who Discovers the Story of Early Man (NF) (illus)	75p
	0426200136	Doctor Who Discovers the Conquerors (NF) (illus)	75p
Δ	0426200632	Junior Doctor Who: Brain of Moribus	90p
	0426116151	TERRANCE DICKS AND MALCOLM HULKE The Making of Doctor Who	95p

STAR Books are obtainable from many booksellers and newsagents. If you have any difficulty please send purchase price plus postage on the scale below to:

Star Cash Sales
P.O. Box 11
Falmouth
Cornwall
OR
Star Book Service,
G.P.O. Box 29,
Douglas,
Isle of Man,
British Isles.

While every effort is made to keep prices low, it is sometimes necessary to increase prices at short notice. Star Books reserve the right to show new retail prices on covers which may differ from those advertised in the text or elsewhere.

Postage and Packing Rate
UK: 40p for the first book, 18p for the second book and 13p for each additional book ordered to a maximum charge of £1·49p. BFPO and EIRE: 40p for the first book, 18p for the second book, 13p per copy for the next 7 books, thereafter 7p per book. Overseas: 60p for the first book and 18p per copy for each additional book.